Treachery Pass

LEE E. WELLS

CENTER POINT LARGE PRINT
THORNDIKE, MAINE

This Center Point Large Print edition
is published in the year 2016 by arrangement with
Golden West Literary Agency.

The text of this Large Print edition is unabridged.
In other aspects, this book may vary
from the original edition.

Set in 16-point Times New Roman type.

ISBN: 978-1-62899-876-4 (hardcover)
ISBN: 978-1-62899-880-1 (paperback)

Library of Congress Cataloging-in-Publication Data

Names: Wells, Lee E., 1907–1982, author.
Title: Treachery pass / Lee. E. Wells.
Description: Center Point Large Print edition. | Thorndike, Maine :
Center Point Large Print, 2016. | ©1964
Identifiers: LCCN 2015043315| ISBN 9781628998764
    (hardcover : alk. paper) |
ISBN 9781628998801 (pbk. : alk. paper)
Subjects: LCSH: Large type books.
Classification: LCC PS3545.E5425 T74 2016 | DDC 813/.54—dc23
LC record available at http://lccn.loc.gov/2015043315

Printed and bound in Great Britain
by TJ International Ltd, Padstow, Cornwall

MIX
Paper from
responsible sources
FSC
www.fsc.org   FSC® C013056

I

It was early spring but the nights remained cold in the high country and the ground mists rose in the valley as the morning sun sent golden, warming shafts of light toward the high jagged peaks that lined the western sky. The cold dawning light reflected on the single line of the railroad that lifted steeply out of State City in an immediate climb to the high pass, like a jagged ax cut in the mountains silhouetted against the clear, steel-like sky.

It was a long and steady grade. Freight trains leaving the sprawling town below crawled up the slope, black smoke belching from the funnel stacks of the locomotives, the long string of cattle and box cars clanking and straining constantly to the laboring pull. A man going at an easy run could keep abreast until the train reached the pass. Then, with a final black belch of triumph, the locomotive dipped to the downward slope and the runner would be left hopelessly behind.

A single curling plume of blue smoke in a heavy patch of bushes a fourth of the way up the slope matched the many hundreds lifting from chimneys in the town below. Just beyond, a trestle spanned a creek burbling and hurrying to the valley below. The bushes and willows hid and encircled a small clearing and the twenty or so tattered, nondescript men.

They moved about, stamping their feet and beating their arms against their bodies. They edged toward the fire that blazed forth needed warmth. Stubbled faces looked pinched, eyes watered, noses dripped. The men shivered in threadbare coats and patched trousers and thin, worn shirts. Matted hair showed beneath the brims of battered hats or escaped through worn holes in the crowns. Of all ages and sizes, the men all bore the unmistakable mark of the shiftless, homeless wanderer.

As the sun rose higher, the brittle chill began to leave the air. There was less scuffling for a place close to the fire, though some still stood with dirty palms stretched toward the flames. Then, limbs and fingers less stiff, some of them moved toward a little cache formed by a sheet of rusted iron resting on two piles of bricks.

One of them, wearing a dirty but warm jacket, squatted before the cache, bringing out the stale bread, the bits of food that had been begged at back doors in the town below. In the iron-hard, unwritten law of the jungle, no man had kept his gleanings for himself but had added them to the common pool. The man placed the items carefully to one side near cracked boots, aware that the other men hungrily watched. He heard a metallic rattle behind him over by the fire as someone brought scoured tin cans and pie plates in which to cook the communal breakfast.

The food all out, the man judged its amount and then turned his head, counting the empty bellies. An ancient Stetson made a sharp shadow across a young, lean face and planed cheeks covered by a golden stubble. Something in thrust of long jaw and wide chin, in the momentary sharp glint of blue eyes, set him apart from the others. He rubbed soiled hands along his jacket.

"Reckon I've seen less divided more ways," he said in a voice that subtly suggested Texas.

"And I've seen more, that's certain," a heavy red-headed man growled. "Hardly enough to keep one man going a full day."

"Have to do—unless some of us promote the grub down there again."

A graybeard shook his head. "No time. The rattler pulls out down there at nine. We can't hit the doors, git back, eat, and catch the westbound."

The young man stood up, passing his hand over his face. He looked tall and thin, though he had wide shoulders and a broad torso that tapered to narrow hips. The coat hung open, revealing a washed-pale blue shirt; worn jeans were tucked into the scuffed boots. He glanced around the ring, seemed to read their wishes, though his eyes narrowed on the scowl of the redhead.

"Well, we'll make do, then. Boil the coffee grounds again, make up a stew with this mess of greens and stuff. A hunk of bread to chew on and—"

"Who gave you the say-so?" the redhead demanded.

The graybeard whined, "Jake, don't cause no trouble."

Jake's bullet head whipped about and he glared, heavy lower lip protruding. With a contemptuous gesture, his thick arm sent the old man stumbling back. The others edged away, except the young man. Jake faced him. "I asked who gave you the say-so?"

"Not rightly no one, comes to that. Last night, neither. Even you."

"There was enough then."

"It'll still share around," the young man said mildly.

Jake grunted. "I say it won't."

Every man now silently watched, judging the two who faced each other over the small pile of food. Jake's pinched eyes made the circle of the men, defying each, and returned to the young man.

"Some ain't heading west," Jake said. "It'll be this afternoon before they have to catch the string east."

"So?" the young man asked mildly.

"So they can go down and mooch their own meal."

"That ain't right!" someone in the group yelled.

Jake swung around, heavy fists doubled. The hoboes shrank back and Jake, with a grunt, turned back again, growling, "That's the way it'll be."

The young man's wide lips had subtly thinned. "Who gave you the say-so?"

Jake's lips pulled down and he lifted a big fist. "That says so."

"It ain't the jungle way," someone muttered.

"It's my way," Jake snapped, bullet head lowered and eyes sharply watching the young man.

The stained Stetson was thumbed back on the head, revealing thick, uncut, corn-gold hair. The sun struck on a high-bridged, long nose and firm lips.

"Jake, you get some of that hot strong coffee in you and you'll feel better—cut that mean morning feeling right out, along with the raw alcohol you drank last night."

"I'll take the coffee, 'Bo. Thanks for nothing. *And* we'll share up my way. Eight of us going west, counting you. Eight of us eat. The rest hit for the town."

"Now that's a point to argue, Jake."

Jake took a menacing step to the young man, his beefy shoulders straining under his ripped brown coat. He asked in heavy sarcasm, "How long you been on the road, 'Bo?"

The blue eyes suddenly clouded with dark memories and the long lips twisted in a moment's pain. Then the young man's face cleared and he

9

shrugged. "Three years. Long enough to know the rule is to share even."

"Long enough to hear of Overland Jake?"

"That you?"

"That's me."

"Yeah, I heard . . . mostly talk of the way he tries to ramrod a jungle. Heard he learned a hard lesson outside of Dodge, though." The blue eyes sparked. "Or did you learn it?"

Jake's face reddened and then he straightened, heavy lips forming a smile, fists opening. His glance flicked at the hoboes who silently and intently watched, a searching and weighing look.

He looked down at the food. "Okay, divide it. . . ."

The young man relaxed; he turned and bent to pick up the pile. Jake's voice roared, "—my way!"

His heavy fingers taloned the collar of the jacket and he jerked the unbuttoned coat down, pinioning the young man's arms. His fist swung, the blow landing alongside of the head, and his opponent fell sprawling. Jake jumped in, swinging back his foot for a kick with his heavy shoes, aimed right at the head.

Arms still tangled, the young man rolled toward Jake and the foot viciously cut air, missing the head. Jake moved fast to catch his balance, aimed another hurried kick. Fingers grabbed his ankle in a steel vise and twisted. Jake went over backward, arms flailing. He struck the ground with a stunning blow and his fingers aimlessly clawed dirt for a moment. Then his head cleared and he came to a crouch, shaking his head.

The young man had finally cleared his arms. He tried to shuck out of the coat, and had succeeded in getting one arm free when Jake catapulted forward, bullet head lowered, arms reaching to grab and enfold his opponent in a crushing bear hug.

The partially free coat swung like a cape over Jake's face, blinding him. A fist slammed into his ribs with the force of a pile driver. Jake's breath whistled out between strained, parted lips. Then the blinding coat was gone.

The young man danced back out of Jake's reach. With a swift jerk he freed the coat and dropped it. Jake straightened and charged again. The young man faded to the right and Jake whirled, fist striking hard and fast. The blow glanced off the ribs and then Jake's fingers taloned into the cloth of the shirt. He tried to jerk the man to him, but his opponent whipped around and the weakened fabric ripped. A fist came out of nowhere and slammed into Jake's jaw. He staggered back and then doubled from a blow to the stomach.

Jake blindly reached and clutched coarse denim, then the leather of a belt. He pulled the man to him and hung on, though fists beat at his ribs. Grunting, Jake snaked an arm around the young man's slender back. His lips pulled back from his teeth as his arm tightened. The young man's fists tried desperately to beat Jake away, but Jake buried his head in the other's chest and his powerful muscles grew taut.

The two fighters whirled about and the ring of watchers broke as the strained and struggling figures staggered into the circle. They moved erratically and blindly. The younger's face looked strained now, as his back inexorably arched to the pressure against his spine. Jake kept his head lowered, levered into the chest, and his shoulders bunched as he exerted increasing pressure. He grunted as a fist slammed into his side, but his hold did not loosen.

They had approached the fire, now down to glowing coals, but neither man was aware of it. Jake shifted his arms slightly and was triumphantly aware that he had the leverage he wanted. He dug in his heels for the final effort that would snap the ribs and bones.

The young man tried to whip around, half moving Jake with him. A booted foot struck a flat boulder that had been used as a fireplace seat by one of the hoboes. The two men went down, rolling toward the fire. Jake's leg and rump struck the embers and fiery pain seared through him. His deadly hug broke as instinctive reaction shot him away from the fire. The young man rolled free, continued to roll to escape the deadly and powerful arms. He stopped, came to his feet in a flowing motion.

Jake, on the far side of the fire, brought his feet under him and came up like a huge bear rearing for an attack. Then both men stopped short, each staring in amazement beyond the other. There was a concerted gasp as the other men realized that their retreat had been invaded.

Nine strangers ringed the clearing. Eight of them wore the rough warm clothing of the puncher or range rider. Each held a leveled Colt, and eight pairs of hard eyes sharply watched the hoboes. The ninth stranger, except for the heavy buckle of the gunbelt that showed at the parting of his long-skirted coat, might have been a business or professional man from the town below. He was much shorter than his companions and yet he instantly dominated.

He smiled at the young man's round-eyed stare. "Go ahead. Our business can wait until you two have settled yours."

No one moved for a long, long moment; the fight had been forgotten. Then the young man found his voice. "Where did you come from?"

"Yonder," the dapper stranger replied easily.

"What do you want?"

"One of you."

"What for? We ain't done nothing."

"That's my business. But the one I pick will know soon enough."

The young man frowned at the leveled guns, back at the stranger. "You're not the law. You've got no business here. Whyn't you leave us alone?"

One of the armed men took an angry stride toward him. The stranger said sharply, "Let it lay, Tag."

The gunman reluctantly settled back on his heels. The stranger studied the young man for a long moment. Suddenly another of the gunmen half turned and his gun roared in the clearing. On the far side, the graybeard yelled, grabbed his ribs. The young man moved swiftly, jumping toward the one who had fired, his lean face tight with anger.

As he came near, the man called Tag spun on his heel and his gun barrel slammed against the back of the young man's skull. He dropped, slack and sprawling.

The dapper stranger said calmly, "Well, two of you have learned your lesson. See if the old coot's bad hit."

"How about the rest of 'em, Brad?"

"Line 'em up."

Tag signaled a gunhawk to look at the old man, who sat clutching his side, blood slowly oozing from between his dirty fingers. Tag made a motion toward the fire with his gun and the subdued and frightened hoboes shuffled over to it. The remaining gunmen held their places. Tag cursed the hoboes into a single line, facing the stranger.

"They're a sad bunch of culls, Brad," Tag said. "Hardly worth the ride—except maybe for that big redhead. Some spunk there."

"But no brains. He's stupid."

Jake flushed and looked angry, but the guns held him with their silent threat. The gunman who had crossed to the old man called, "He'll live. Gouged along his rib, that's all. Want him over with the rest?"

"Let him sit," Brad Moran answered. "But watch him—and the others."

He adjusted his flat-crowned black hat and came forward now. He looked sharply at the first hobo and, without comment, moved on to the next, passed him with a shake of the head. The third he ordered, with a slight jerk of his hand, to step out. Frightened and uncertain, the man moved up, halted when a gun muzzle half lifted toward him.

Moran went on down the line. By the time he reached the far end three had been motioned to step out—one of them Jake. Moran returned to the three, stepped back and considered them, frowning. Not a sound broke the stillness of the clearing. Moran shook his head slightly and then turned to the sprawled body of the young man.

"Turn him over, Tag."

Tag holstered his gun, bent and with rough carelessness rolled the unconscious man over onto his back. Brad looked down into the long, lean face, roughened with sun and wind, with little crow's-feet at the corners of the closed eyes. He studied the slender but muscular body, the worn boots.

He broke the silence. "Bring him around."

Tag knelt beside the man, lifted him and began methodically slapping his face. The head rolled limply from side to side with each smacking blow. Then the body stiffened and the man made a faint protesting sound of pain. Suddenly the eyes snapped open, looked blankly around. They settled on Tag and then the stranger who stood calmly nearby. The young man jerked into a sitting position.

Moran said, "Stand up."

The young man glared and then read the harsh determination on the faces of the armed men. He came slowly to his feet and stood painfully rubbing his skull where the gun barrel had clipped him. Moran thumbed back his hat and slowly, carefully considered his captive.

"What's your name?"

"What's it matter?"

"Nothing, except as a brand. You do have a name?"

A slight shrug. "Ballard . . . Ken Ballard."

"Okay, Ken. Where you from?"

"You're damn nosey."

"I intend to be. You can take it easy or hard, however you want."

Ken's wide lips thinned but he answered grudgingly, "South, mostly."

"Now what does that mean?"

Ken's lips set tight, as though to refuse further

answer. Moran was not a tall man, but he exuded a strong and dangerous magnetism. Ken looked into ice-gray eyes that had a strange habit of flicking from side to side, yet still held in a demanding stare. He sensed the ruthlessness beneath the smooth exterior, borne out by the hard-faced armed men who took Moran's orders.

Ken said, "South—New Mexico, Arizona, Texas—take your choice."

Moran's pale face looked subtly pleased. "Puncher, then. So you can ride a horse and maybe handle a four or six team?"

"I've done it."

"How about a gun?"

"Let me have one and I'll show you."

Moran grinned. "Not yet. Running from the law?"

"No."

"What, then?"

"You find out."

"I will." Brad Moran turned to Tag. "This one. Leave the others."

He turned on his heel and strode across the clearing to a narrow path. Tag tapped Ken on the shoulder and indicated the way his boss had gone. "Shift your boots, friend. You're going with us."

Ken shook his head. "Now wait a minute. What's this all about?"

"You'll find out. Git moving."

"Not me. I'm catching the westbound freight."

Tag rubbed his hand on his holster, lifted it to the gun handle. "I got a bullet says you're not."

Their eyes locked and Ken read the truth in the thin, smiling lips and narrowed eyes. He turned and slowly crossed the clearing, Tag immediately behind him.

II

When Ken Ballard broke through the screen of bushes hiding the jungle, he stopped short in surprise. Some yards ahead of him, Moran marched toward a dozen ground-tied horses, watched by another rider of the same breed as Tag and the others. Only the fight with Jake had prevented the suspicious eyes and ears of the hoboes from being aware of the approach of such a cavalcade.

Behind Ken, Tag's harsh voice said, "One of those broncs is for you. Think you can fork it?"

Ken did not reply, but moved on. Ahead, Moran took the reins of a rangy bay and swung into the saddle with practiced ease. He settled and then pulled a short thin cigar from his vest pocket. As he struck a match and lit the cigar, he watched Ken approach. As Ken came up, Moran indicated a paint cow pony. "That one's for you."

Ken walked to the animal and, under Moran's watchful eyes, mounted. Now Ken saw that Tag and the other men had left the jungle. Beyond them he could see Jake, the wounded old man, and some of the others peering cautiously out with frightened curiosity. There was a moment of milling and then all the gunmen were mounted.

Moran lifted his reins but Ken said harshly, "I

don't know what this is all about, but I know damn well it's kidnaping."

Moran smiled coldly. "Is there anyone but you who cares?"

Ken's lean face tightened and his eyes grew bleak and hurt. Moran grinned more widely and, without a word, reined about. He rode off, the rest of the men following. Tag jerked his thumb at Ken, who lifted the reins and kicked the paint into motion.

To Ken's faint surprise, they did not head for the town. Moran set his horse northward, paralleling the mountain range to their left. After a time, Tag motioned two of the men to close up on either side of Ken; then Tag cantered up beside Moran. The two of them rode some distance ahead. They talked, but Ken could not heard the words.

Anger still rode him but, yard by yard, it died under the onslaught of curiosity. He sensed now that there would be no violence unless he brought it on himself. The cavalcade around him proved that Brad Moran was a man of some substance and power. The fine coat, the black hat, the white shirt and black silk tie the man wore indicated money. What would a man like that want with a drifting bum picked up out of a hobo jungle?

The miles dropped behind them. Now and then one of the riders would say a short word to a companion, but for the most part there was no talk. They came to a road that Ken judged led

20

from the town, now far behind them, up over the mountains to the west. Moran and Tag turned into it, and now the riders began the climb to the high peaks.

The road plunged into a canyon where trees showed the first spring swelling on bare branches. Ken heard distant sounds—the rattle of chains and the roll of heavy wheels. The riders moved to one side of the road without breaking pace. Soon a stagecoach wheeled around a bend, passed—with the driver giving them a startled look—and disappeared behind them.

A short distance further, the canyon opened onto a mountain valley. Moran reined off the road to a pleasant, sun-dappled space between high trees. He swung out of saddle, and Ken knew that the preliminaries to this strange game were over.

He dismounted, turned to find Moran facing him, some distance away. Tag and the other riders stood by their horses, grim, their attention centered on Ken. Brad Moran broke the short tense silence. "Rest your saddles, boys. Tag, you and I can talk to our new friend here. Break out some coffee. We could all use some."

"And some chow," Ken said half defiantly. "You might've had breakfast. I didn't."

Moran made a short signal to one of the men, who turned to the pack horse he had led all the way from the jungle. The men moved about then, gathering firewood, lighting cigarettes. Moran motioned Ken to follow him and led the way to a fallen tree. He sat down upon the trunk and Ken took a stand a few steps before him.

Each man studied the other as if they had just met, a new appraisal and a weighing. Ken looked down on a fairly short man, but one with wide shoulders and strong arms, and with the vitality and magnetism, the confidence of someone a foot taller. Brad Moran had a face that just missed being moon shaped, and skin almost wholly without color. But the pale skin had an inner glow. His mouth was small and his lips thin, and the upper lip peaked over the lower at the center. Now that he had removed his hat, Ken could see that his hair was black, straight and a bit long at the neck.

He had unbuttoned the long-skirted coat and Ken saw the fine gray cloth of the suit coat, and the costly vest. A gunbelt circled Moran's waist, the pliant leather of the holster holding a blue steel gun snugly to the hip. The gray trousers covered the tops of short boots that reflected polished light even after what was obviously a long journey.

He had a soft voice, almost without inflection, as subtly strange as those shifting eyes. "Ballard— Ken Ballard—from the border country. Is that it?"

"That's it."

"Been a puncher. I know you can ride. Pretty

good fighter, from what I saw. Claim you can handle a gun. Not running from the law."

He paused as though waiting for confirmation, but Ken said nothing. After a moment Moran asked sharply, "What made you a bum?"

"That's none of your business."

Tag half rose from his seat, mean eyes alight, but Moran made a negative sign. Tag eased back but scowled as Moran said, "If you want it that way. Makes no difference. But I'll guess. Someone gunning for you . . . drink . . . a woman."

He watched sharply as he spoke, and caught the slight flick of Ken's expression on the last word. Moran made no comment, merely asked, "How long have you been without a saddle?"

"About three years."

"Tired of it?"

Ken hesitated, a new light flaring and then dying in his eyes. He heard the crackle of flames behind him, the rattle of pots. He moistened his lips, feeling his stomach quiver emptily. He shoved hunger aside so he could face the problem of the man before him.

"You ride in circles, mister."

After a second, Moran nodded. "All right, perhaps I do. I'll give you a chance to get on your feet again and hold your head up."

Ken's lips moved in a cynical grin. "Santa Claus clean out of season! You're just a generous gent who goes around with a pack of gun wolves, kidnaping bums to make 'em happy! You still ride in circles, mister. And, by the way, who are you?"

Tag growled, "Brad, I wanta break some of his teeth."

Moran laughed. "Let him be. He stacks up more and more to what we want." He sobered. "Ever been in this country before?"

"Nope, and I'm not likely to come again."

"Likely you've never heard of Brad Moran, then."

"Nope, and right now I'd like to forget him—after some coffee and chow."

"I own and operate the Moran Freight Lines."

"Never heard of that, either."

Moran's lips thinned. "Ballard, you'll learn that I allow a man only so much rope. You're tugging on the end of yours now."

Tag looked eager, a big man with a rocky, high-boned face, the skin a dark red and pulled tight over a craggy jaw. His eyes shadowed with disappointment as Ken shrugged and refused the challenge.

Brad Moran continued after a pause. "Ballard, you're going to work for me."

"Maybe."

"How far have we ridden?" Moran asked sharply.

"Oh, maybe ten miles."

"Ten miles from nowhere. I brought you here to offer a job that I think you'll fit. I don't have to take you back where I found you. I could leave you here and—" Moran's round face became quietly menacing—"who'd look for a missing bum up here clean off the road? Who'd care much, if they found a dead one around here sometime in the next year?"

Ken's lips pursed and he said in soft wonder, "I think you mean that."

"You can find out—or you can take the job."

"What is it?"

"Driving a freight wagon."

"That all?"

"Making a report now and then to me or to Nixon." He indicated Tag. "Following orders."

"Then I'll not be working for you."

"You'll be drawing pay from me—and someone else. Before that, however, you'll get decent clothes, regular food, and a few drinks. You'll drive one of my wagons for a month or so. I think that's a fair deal. Will you take it?"

Ken thoughtfully rubbed his hand along his jaw and his stomach tightened at the smell of coffee and bacon from the fire behind him. He spoke slowly. "You're not showing two hole cards—who I'll work for and what's in it for you."

"I don't intend to—now. You take this job a step at a time or not at all."

"All legal?"

"Driving a freight wagon—what's wrong with that?"

"And making reports," Ken added sharply.

"Find a law against it," Moran snapped.

Ken settled back on his heels. Moran and Tag watched him closely but he disregarded them. His mind turned over the many aspects of the deal. He had a lot of questions to ask but he knew Moran would not answer them. As near as he could see, he would be a spy for Moran, and that meant he would work for a competing freight line.

Unethical, Ken thought, but what part of the last three years had been ethical? He saw a series of vivid mental pictures—freight cars, hobo jungles, now and then an odd job, when he had one of those periods of wanting to be something again. But they always ended the same way; someone tricked him, doublecrossed him. No one could be trusted. He had learned that when— He saw the soft, beautiful lips of a woman forming acid words, marking him as a fool, a baling-wire rancher with dreams too big for his abilities.

Ken's eyes spasmodically closed and he was unaware that Moran shot a questioning, meaningful look at Tag Nixon.

Ken fought down the memories. But Moran's strange offer and the need for decision had opened the past. Not coherently, but in flashing scenes jumping here and there over time and space. The swinging hickory clubs of railroad bulls—in Dodge, that was . . . the old dying bum in a freight car rattling in the high canyons of New Mexico, clutching blindly at Ken's shirt . . . a gambling table, and his last chip going into the pot as he reached for the whiskey that dulled the pain. The last chip—and then it was gone. He saw himself standing up, swaying a moment and then walking out—to wander from that moment to this.

His eyes focused again and he became aware of Moran's pale face, Tag's hard stare. He smelled coffee and bacon again and he lifted his dirty hands to look at them. His shirt was ripped; his boots were wearing out. He felt his unshaven chin—and when had he last had a chance to bathe?

Ken moistened his lips, feeling deep within him the urge to escape from wandering and squalor. Moran offered that chance, though there were things about the offer that Ken did not like. But so long as the job offered the means, why question the ends? It was legal, Moran had said; that was enough. Here was a chance to be a man again, to rebuild what someone else had destroyed. There might not be another chance.

Moran said softly, "Well?"

Ken took a deep breath. "I'll try it."

"Oh, no! All the way, right from the beginning. I'm not throwing away money and time on you."

Ken hesitated a second longer. Then the inner urge came up strong and he blurted, "Okay. You've hired a hand."

Moran studied him for a long moment, his strange eyes probing. Then he placed his hands on his knees and stood up, satisfied. "You're working for me this minute, Ballard. Tag will tell you what I expect from my men."

He circled Ken and walked to the fire. Ken turned, eager for food and the hot coffee. He had taken a step when a hand fell on his shoulder. He was whirled around, had a startled glimpse of Tag's tight face. Then a fist smashed into his jaw and lights flashed before his eyes as he fell.

He struck the ground heavily. The shock of it cleared his brain and he started to scramble to his feet. He froze when he looked up into the black muzzle of a gun and Tag Nixon's mean eyes, just as deadly, above it.

"Nothing personal, Ballard. Brad wanted me to teach you how it'll be."

Ken touched his aching jaw and slowly stood up. Tag kept the gun lined on him. "Brad works this way. You do what you're told or you get hurt. If that don't work, this will."

He slightly tilted the gun muzzle. Then, with a flowing motion, he dropped the Colt into his holster. "Now let's get something to eat. We got a long way to ride."

He circled Ken and walked unconcernedly to the fire.

III

The ride, Ken Ballard learned, was a two-day one. They crossed the mountain range and headed northwest toward another line of peaks along the distant horizon. They ignored a cowtown except to purchase supplies there, and pitched camp at night. After they had climbed the second range, Ken judged they were not too far from the Montana Territory line. They came down into rolling country, good range land, and Brad led the way with the undeviating steadiness of a homing pigeon.

Then, far to the north, Ken saw another line of mountains. The riders came on a road, turned into it and followed it for many miles. Suddenly Ken sighted a rail line off to the right, bisecting the road and heading north and west. Shortly after, he saw the houses and buildings of a fair-sized town ahead.

It proved to be their destination. They rode down the main dirt street of the town, and Ken noticed that those along the street watched with only mild curiosity. He wondered how often Brad Moran appeared at the head of so many riders. A man wearing a marshal's badge waved casually to Moran without breaking his easy stride. So, Ken thought—the law in this town belongs to Brad Moran.

At the far end of the street stood a huge freight yard, the gates open to the street. Moran turned in, angled toward a small door marked "Office," and dismounted. At Tag's slight signal, Ken followed, swung out of saddle and ground tied the paint. As Moran stepped into the office, a lanky man rose from a rolltop desk beyond a rail barrier. Two male clerks at a high desk glanced up briefly from under green eyeshades.

Moran pushed open the swing door in the barrier, motioned Ken forward. "Put this man on the station payroll, Ott."

"What job?" the lanky man asked. He had a long sallow face with deep wrinkles, and his mouth pulled down in an ugly curve at the corners. "We got plenty of help."

"Make room. I want Ballard broken in here. Later I'll take him to Pass City." Moran considered Ken. "Let him learn how to load, if he doesn't already know. Put him on town freight for a couple of weeks, then out on a regular run—helper first, then driver."

Ott shot a glance at Ken, then looked back at Moran. "If you say so, Brad."

"I say so. Oh, his name's Ken Ballard. Get him a complete new outfit of clothes and advance him enough money to live until his first payday. Regular wages, Ott."

"Less what he'll owe for the extras?"

"No, charge them to me personal." Moran

turned directly to Ken, though he spoke the words to the station manager. "I have plans for this'n, Ott. But show him no favors. I want to find out if he's worth a damn. Let me know about him when you send in the weekly reports."

"If he don't work out?"

"Just let me know." Moran's shifting eyes for once held steady and cold on Ken's. "Tag or one of the boys will be down to take care of it. He's a drifter, Ott, and no one will come looking for him if . . ."

His voice drifted off and a short silence settled on the office. Then one of the clerks moved uneasily and the deadly tension was broken.

By nightfall, Ken had a few coins in the pockets of his stiff new jeans and the new wool shirt felt comfortable to his back. His new boots felt a little stiff, but they'd work out all right. His stomach was full and he had rented a little two-room shack on a side street at the edge of town.

Moran and Tag disappeared sometime in the afternoon but Ott told Ken to report ready for work in the morning, setting a time just at dawn. Ken read the curiosity in the manager's eyes but the man asked no questions. Ken began to realize the kind of organization Moran had built up.

But he gave little thought to it that night. He luxuriated in walking about the town after another full meal. He hesitated before one of the saloons, but finally went in. He had a single drink, wanted more, but recalled what had happened the last time he had surrendered to desire. Unused to much whiskey of late, the single shot hit and exploded like a warm bomb. Warning enough.

So he returned to the dark street and walked along toward the shack he had left just at sundown. He heard a train whistle and halted in midstride. It whistled again, closer, and then beyond the buildings he heard the train's rush through the town, the final mournful whistle sounding back as it hurried northward.

Ken walked on, thinking someone he knew might be riding the tender of that locomotive, half frozen and miserable, wandering out of nowhere and going nowhere. He shivered as though he, too, felt the biting teeth of the cold wind through a tattered coat.

Nor did the chill disappear until he had lit the lamp in the shack and the warm yellow glow filled the small, ugly room. But it was a home, a room— not a bouncing freight car or a miserable jungle. He wondered at how swiftly revulsion had come for the life he had just left, then cast that thought aside as he looked at the narrow cot and the blankets. How long had it been!

Dawn was just streaking the east the next morning when Ken turned in the wide gates of the station. He stopped short in surprise at the activity. Three big freight wagons had been backed up to the warehouse and he had to jump aside as another bounced emptily through the gates and headed toward the railroad station.

Within minutes, Ken, coat off, was laboring with a dozen others, loading a wagon which had replaced one of the three that had lumbered off. The light grew stronger, but Ken hardly noticed, except to be grateful. He wrestled crates, boxes, barrels from stacks on the warehouse floor into the big bed of the wagon. Sweat streamed in his eyes and his muscles ached and protested against the unaccustomed labor. The wagon rolled off, the driver carrying a sheaf of manifests. Another driver, with lurid blasphemy at his team, backed his wagon in its place and demanded that it be filled.

And then the wagon Ken had seen go out returned, heavily loaded. He was assigned by a cursing foreman to help unload, and the cargo was broken up and stacked according to destination. When Ken had rolled the last barrel out of the wagon, there was a lull. The warehousemen instantly pulled off their gloves and lit pipes. Ken dropped exhausted on a low crate and considered his blistered, cut hands; he pulled a splinter out of a finger.

This morning was to prove to be but the introduction to the rest of the day and the week. But that first night, Ken walked painfully home, every muscle aching. His single drink at the saloon didn't help much and it was an effort to cook a simple meal, blow out the lamp and drop into bed. He wondered for a moment if the new life was worth the exhaustion but, before he could find an answer, he had fallen into a drugged sleep.

He pulled himself, aching, from bed at dawn. So it went all week, but each day was a little easier than the one before. He began to get a picture of the freighting business. From this railhead all the surrounding smaller towns' merchants and many ranches were served by Moran's wagons. He had a monopoly in the area and, as Ken had time to talk to his companions, he learned that Brad Moran was one of the giants in the freighting business.

But there was no warmth to the business, Ken swiftly learned. Every bit of equipment, every horse, even every worker had been judged for work capacity to the hilt, and that was demanded. Not that Ken cared, for the moment. He ate, he had a few drinks, he had shelter. That was enough.

Late Saturday, Ken fell in line with the rest of the workers for his pay. For once the station yard was without bustle as the queue of drivers, helpers, stablemen and loaders snaked across the yard to the office door. Looking through the big gates onto the street, Ken saw riders from the nearby ranches pass by on their way to stores and saloons. For all its size, this was basically a cowtown. Ken felt a stir of excitement, a wish to mingle. He had almost forgotten the feeling.

When he stepped into the office and up to the rail, Ott looked up from a table, and extended a slip of paper showing the wages due. Ken signed, and Ott counted the coins from the neat stacks before him. Ken swept up his pay and started to turn, but Ott checked him.

"Ballard, think you've learned to load a wagon so the cargo won't shift?"

"I got some of the hang, anyhow."

"Monday morning I'm putting you on the town wagon. We'll see if you've learned."

Ken nodded, pocketed the coins and left the office. Outside the station, he strolled along the street, fingers jingling the coins in his pocket. Three years and more, he thought, since he'd actually earned, rather than scrounged, any money. No need to panhandle for a cup of coffee now. He could walk into any store, any saloon, with his head up.

The excitement he had first felt increased. The crowd along the sidewalk jostled him but he liked the feel of it. There was only one thing wrong—he was alone and not with a ranch crew, as he had been on those Saturday nights long ago. He came to a saloon and turned in, boot heels rapping firmly on the wooden porch, hand striking wide the batwings with a new assurance, a sense of belonging.

That feeling lasted through the first drink, over which he lingered, and then began to disappear with the second. He was one of many men who lined the bar. Talk and noise beat at him, men inadvertently pressed against him. He was one of a crowd, but no one paid any attention to him beyond incurious glances that took him in and then dismissed him. No one spoke to him except the bartender, disinterestedly sweeping in the coins for his drinks.

Ken looked at his reflection in the mirror, then at the uncaring men about him. He felt a growing sense of loneliness, of not belonging. Friends, comrades, saddle partners—where did they belong? In the past, and there they'd stay.

He ordered a third drink, feeling the effect of the first two. But he grimly sought relief from the sense of being an outcast. It began to come with the fourth drink. By then he knew that he didn't need friends and companions. He should remember the lesson the past had taught him—depend on someone at your own risk. Especially a woman . . . oh, especially!

Pushing from the bar, he turned and walked gravely to the distant batwings, the lamp lights fuzzy, the floor not exactly stationary. He stepped out on the dark porch and took a deep breath of the chill air. He looked down at the moving crowd along the sidewalk, feeling superior in his acid knowledge. Now he understood his basic mistake; he must ride his trail alone, not take someone with him as he had tried to do before.

He nodded, pleased with his newfound wisdom.

Take what comes; like this job, but take it just for yourself. Try to share it and you give it all away, or it's taken from you. He squared his shoulders, set his hat more firmly and with precise, careful movements descended the few wide steps to the street.

Ken went to work with relief on Monday morning, glad that the empty hours of Sunday were behind him. He reported to Ott, who indicated a team of horses in the stable and an empty light wagon in the yard. The manager watched until Ken had almost completed hitching up the horses, then he left with a grunt of satisfaction.

Later, in the office, Ken received instructions and shortly after rattled out onto the street, heading for the depot and small freight station. He labored there with his helper, a wiry silent man named Monty, and then drove away, the horses straining to the load.

That started the day. The work was not quite so steadily strenuous as the week before, but by nightfall Ken's muscles still ached. Each day's program was the same: loads from depot to station, pick up shipments of varying sizes from the merchants and take them to the station for later delivery to outlying mines and small towns. Deliver shipments to town merchants. Back to the station to unhitch the team and turn them over to the stable hostlers.

Late one afternoon, Ken drove up to the station warehouse and helped unload. The wagon bed emptied and checked with the manifests, he took a small package from the seat and placed it on some small boxes assigned to a distant village. The foreman looked questioningly at him.

"What's that?"

"Some dresses the lady at the hardware store made for a friend."

"What're you doing with it?"

Ken shrugged. "She made 'em for her friend— wife of the man who gets these." He indicated the boxes. "Asked if I'd see it went along with the shipment."

The foreman glanced at a shipping memo. "You didn't list it."

"Why? It's just a favor."

"You work for Moran. We don't do any favors, Ballard."

"But that won't take any room!"

"Not the point. We'll be hauling it for nothing. If we start that, there's no ending."

Ken frowned, puzzled. "But the hardware store gives us all their business. I figured this'd sort of thank 'em."

"For what? Who else will haul for 'em?" The foreman judged the box. "I'll add two bits to the bill. That'll about cover it. Just don't do something like this again."

Ken shrugged, turned away. A further aspect of

Brad Moran's character, he thought—another view of his cold, impersonal business methods. But then, Moran also rode his trail alone, something Ken had but recently learned to do.

In the following month and more, Ken held many jobs. He took the long hauls, as helper and driver. He became hostler at the main station and then for a week at a small cowtown, the terminal of one of the routes. He was pulled back to the main station and had the town wagon again.

He began to wonder what had happened to the plans Moran had for him, whatever they were. Ott made no mention of Moran and neither the boss nor his gun-carrying shadow, Tag Nixon, appeared. Ken began to wonder if Moran had changed his mind and he would be forgotten. Not that he cared. If that happened, he could leave the job when he tired of it.

Spring advanced and the days grew warm, the nights cool but pleasant. Ken's life became a routine between the station, a single drink at the saloon, then to his shack for a lonely meal and sleep. Now his muscles had toughened and his body had adjusted to the heavy work. With the lessening of strain, the increased familiarity with the job, came a growing urge to move on to new scenes. Three years of wandering had left its mark on him and often he found himself listening longingly to the whistle of the night train as it roared into the town and out. The distant, echoing wail in the far passes called to him with a lonely nostalgia.

The feeling increased as the days grew warmer and longer and each morning he had to force himself to make the short walk to the station. Each morning it grew harder, and he knew that soon he would catch one of the freights, swing up in an empty box car and let the locomotive take him yonderly.

It was particularly hard one morning. He paused on a corner. Turn left and he could walk to the railroad. Go straight ahead and he'd be wrestling crates and boxes. He rubbed his hands along his trousers, his eyes distant, his body tense with the inner struggle. Finally he walked on, straight ahead.

When he jumped up on the loading dock, the foreman called, "Ballard, they want you at the office."

Ken jumped back off the dock and slowly crossed the yard. When he opened the office door, he saw Tag Nixon standing near Ott's inner office. Nixon's hard eyes swept over Ken. The heavy face did not change expression; only the pinched eyes showed a faint approval.

"Well, you've changed considerable," he said heavily.

"Good, clean hard work," Ken grunted, and Nixon grinned.

"That's what I hear." He indicated the office. "I want to talk to you."

Ott stood near the railing, watching, and made no move to join them. When Ken had stepped into the cubicle of an office, Nixon closed the door. He stood there, again weighing Ken. Finally he waved to a chair and himself dropped into Ott's seat behind the scarred desk.

"From Ott's reports," the gunman said abruptly, "Brad figures you're ready for the job he has in mind."

"I wondered if you'd forgotten."

"Not Brad—or me. Brad always gets his money's worth. You should know by now."

Ken nodded, waited. Nixon again considered him. "Do you figure now you could get a job anywhere as a hand with a freight outfit?"

"I've learned."

Nixon glanced at the closed door and his heavy voice lowered slightly. "I've told Ott we're transferring you to Pass City. That's where you'll go, but you'll not work for us."

"Who, then?"

"You'll know in time." Nixon pulled money from his pocket and held it out. "Here's railroad fare to Pass City. Catch tomorrow's train. When you get there, go to the Red Cloud Hotel and get a room."

Ken slowly accepted the money. "Then what?"

"Hang around and stay sober until you hear

from me. That won't be long." He stood up. "Above all, don't say anything about having worked for Brad Moran—anywhere. Got that?"

"Sure."

"You'll get orders from me or Brad. Right now, that's all you need to know. See you in Pass City."

He opened the door and walked out. Ken slowly followed. Nixon left the main office but Ott signaled Ken over and extended a pay slip for him to sign. "Through tonight, Ballard. But you'd better go home, get packed, and wind things up here."

Ken signed, accepted the money, counted it and his brow arched as he asked, "Has Moran gone soft? He's paying me for not working."

Ott tucked the signed receipt away. "One way or another, you'll pay for it, Ballard. It always works that way."

IV

The moment Ken stepped off the train at Pass City, he knew why Moran had made it his headquarters. Two railroads served the town, one from the south and one from the east. Ken's train had rattled for some distance between cattle pens and switching yards. From the station platform he could see three large freight depots and, circling the building, he looked far down a business street filled with wagons, buckboards, heavy freight wagons. There was bustle and size to Pass City; it was a minor metropolis.

Getting directions from the station master, Ken found the Red Cloud Hotel. It was a high, narrow building a few blocks away, sandwiched between a café and a saloon, both squat structures with high false fronts. The lobby had seen better days; the few leather chairs were cracked, everything was dusty including the mustached, limping clerk who wheezed as he gave Ken the key.

The afternoon and night passed with no word from Nixon or Moran. Ken remained close to the hotel most of the next morning, stretched out on the bed or seated by the window watching the heavy traffic in the street below. When there was still no contact by noon, irritated, he decided to see something of the town.

He wandered about the nearby streets and inadvertently came on the Moran depot. The stables, yard, and warehouses stretched solidly along the block, making the station Ken had just left seem small, almost insignificant. He crossed to the far side of the street and examined the place as he walked along. The heavy wagons with the usual red M painted on the high sideboards were lined at the loading docks. Ken stood for long moments looking through the high wide-open gates into the yard. There was an activity here exceeding anything he had known before.

He saw many men bustling about and, through the office windows, clerks at high desks. But there was no sight of Moran or his gunhawk. Ken finally moved along and stepped into a nearby saloon.

The place was small and he the only customer. He ordered a drink and then indicated the big warehouse, almost across the street. "As big a freighting outfit as I've ever seen."

"Moran? Real big—and growing all the time." The bartender, glad of company, moved down near Ken. "Everything south of here goes and comes in Moran wagons—nothing else."

"That's a lot of country. You'd think there'd be others."

"There was, five years ago. But Brad Moran bought 'em out or run 'em out. In some cases he cut hauling prices down to where he lost money for a year or more. The little outfits went broke and had to fold up."

"Sounds hard and tough," Ken commented.

"That's what Moran is." The bartender refilled Ken's glass. "On the house, friend. There ain't only drivers and such on Moran's payroll. There's hardcases. Now and then they come in here, and you can tell they know how to use the guns they wear."

"A crew like that sounds like a shady outfit."

"Well, I wouldn't say that. Moran's stations are scattered all over to the south. Now and then there's been outlaws, or trouble of one kind or another. I reckon the gunslingers sort of keep things in line."

"You keep talking about the south. No shipping north?"

The bartender chuckled. "Not for Moran. He ain't found a way to buck Hanes."

"Hanes?"

"Lou Hanes. Him and Moran is as different as day from night. Folks like Lou. They do business with Moran because they have to, but they don't like him."

"Then this Hanes ought to move south," Ken grunted.

"Well, Lou never did do much down there. He always worked north of the Treachery Range. Come in here years ago when the railroads first built through. Lot of little freighters then—one-wagon outfits. No one had an idea of grabbing everything off, especially Lou. He's one who believes in live and let live."

The man indicated the empty glass but Ken shook his head. "Not yet, thanks. Then north there's several outfits?"

"Just Lou, now. Worked out that way—oh, ten years ago. Lou's just as ambitious as Moran, but he's fair and square. He bought some out. Others sort of faded, because people up that way trusted Lou from the beginning. The larger he grew, the more they turned to him for hauling and freighting."

"And now Moran's stopped cold?"

"Well, right now at least. But I wouldn't gamble on how long. Moran tried it up there; he went in, but he got no business. Then he tried cutting prices like he did before. Only a few shippers fell for it. Most of 'em figured prices would shoot higher'n a bronc's back once Moran got hold. They did down south."

Ken thoughtfully rubbed his jaw, beginning to get a glimmer of his place in Moran's plans. "So Hanes has it all to himself for good?"

"Moran tried buying Lou out, I heard. Nothing came of that. Then a couple of Lou's wagons was robbed."

"Moran?"

"No proof of that. Just happened. Anyhow, Hanes has a young troubleshooter superintendent,

Frank Sparks, who can move mighty fast. Frank trailed the outlaws. Killed two of them, and the rest are still running, I reckon."

"Are those two Moran's?"

"Same breed of gundog, but no one ever found a connection with Moran's outfit. No, I wouldn't say they were."

Ken indicated his glass for a refill. "So now the whole country is divided by two freighters— Moran and Hanes. Sort of a Mexican stand-off."

"That's about it. I hope it stays that way. If one'd move in on the other, there'd be a lot of gunplay. I know Lou won't. He ain't that kind. But Moran . . ."

"Funny thing," Ken commented, "here you get the business from Moran's outfit, but I'd say you don't like him."

The bartender brushed his towel over the bar top. "Friend, a pig makes good ham, but do you have to love the pig?"

Ken laughed, dropped money on the bar and left. Outside, he studied the long expanse of the freighting station, seeing it now in the light of what he had just heard. Absently he rubbed his hand along his right hip, then realized what he was doing. His eyes grew distant and grim. Would he soon wear a gun there as part of his job for Moran?

He turned on his heel and strode away. Curious now, asking directions, he soon came on another freighting station. A long sign over a low building to one side of the gates read "Hanes—Freighter." It was not nearly as large as Moran's nor, at the moment, did it seem as busy. There were no wagons loading, but Ken knew most of them would already be rolling heavily toward their destinations.

From what he could see of the yard, it was neat and orderly. He heard the muffled clang of a blacksmith's hammer from somewhere beyond the high street fence. Suddenly a woman appeared in the yard, walking briskly toward one of the buildings.

Ken watched. She was tall, slender. He became aware of dark red hair piled high on the proud head, saw a clean and delicate profile. She carried papers and walked swiftly with a graceful stride out of Ken's sight beyond the gate. She had appeared and disappeared so swiftly that he had little more than a fleeting impression of stately beauty.

He also had an impulse to wait for her return so that he could see her again. That surprised him; it was three years since he had looked at a woman with anything but distrust and dislike. He turned abruptly on his heel and strode away, half angry with himself.

The rest of the day and the evening passed without word. Returning to the hotel after breakfast the next morning, Ken opened the door to his room and stopped short. Tag Nixon lolled on the bed. He swung his heavy legs around and off as Ken recovered from his surprise and closed the door.

Ken dropped his hat on the rickety dresser, pulled out the single chair and sat down. Nixon waited expectantly for a long moment, then broke the silence. "You look like you've had long enough rest."

"I'm tired of loafing."

Nixon chuckled. "Now that's something, coming from a bum."

Ken's lean cheeks flushed and he said tightly, "I wondered when you'd come."

"In good time—mine and Brad's. Now we're ready, so you go to work."

"Doing what?"

Nixon leaned to one side to pull some currency from his pocket. He counted off several bills and extended them. "First you buy a horse and saddle, get some grub and a bedroll."

"I'm traveling, then?"

Nixon made an impatient gesture with the money and Ken slowly took it. The gunman nodded. "North, up over the Treachery Range."

"For what?"

"I'll come to that. Along with the other stuff, buy yourself a gun and belt. I heard you say you could use a gun."

"Like any puncher, I reckon. But I'm not your kind of gun-hand."

Nixon nodded, pleased. "You don't have to be. Just so you can aim and shoot."

"At who?"

Nixon snapped, "At no one. Oh, and get yourself a blacksnake whip."

"And what do I do with it?"

"Well, on the way, you can practice using it. A whip tied to your saddle proves you're a freighter better than all the arguments you can give. That's what you're going to be—a driver."

Ken placed the money on the dresser beside his hat as Nixon continued. "Thirty miles beyond Treachery Pass is Sioux Springs. That's where you're headed. You'll ride in, look around the town like you're aiming to settle or work there. Then, when the right time comes, you'll get a job driving. There's a freight station—"

"Hanes Freight Lines," Ken cut in.

Nixon's eyes narrowed. "That's right. But how did you know?"

"Just a guess. But Hanes freights everything over the Treachery Range, I hear. Moran hasn't been able to get so much as a toehold so far, they tell me. That right?"

Nixon hesitated, then reluctantly nodded. "How much have you been nosin' around?"

"No more'n anyone with time on his hands." Ken smiled without mirth. "If you didn't want me to know a few things, you should've shown up sooner."

Nixon's heavy jaw set; then he shrugged slightly. "All right, you go to Hanes. None of that outfit knows you're with us. That's why we broke you in on the job over a hundred miles south. When the signal comes, you go to Hanes and get a job driving."

Ken glanced at the money on the dresser. "Horse, saddle, Colt—then a job with Hanes. I know Moran wants the business up there—but bad enough to hire me to gun down Hanes?"

Nixon jumped to his feet. "What makes you think that?"

Ken stood up to face the man. "It adds up, from where I stand. But you bet your money on the wrong hole card. I don't do any killing."

Nixon glared. Then he suddenly laughed and dropped back on the bed. "Hell, for a bum you sure think a lot of yourself! Sit down and calm your feathers."

Ken glared at him, both relieved and angry. He sank onto the chair again and Nixon chuckled mirthlessly before he spoke. "You get the job, that's all. You get it when the time's right."

"When will that be?"

Nixon leaned forward. "There'll be some trouble—for Hanes. When you hear of it, go after a driving job. Right away, understand?"

"What kind of trouble?"

"You'll know when it happens."

"I know what I'm to do and when I'm to do it. But I don't know why."

Nixon stood up and shoved his hat on his head. "Something you ain't learned yet, working for Moran. You don't know why about nothing until you're told."

"What happens after I get the job?"

"I'll meet you from time to time along the roads. You tell me who's shipping, how many wagons, and where. We want to know their business."

"A spy," Ken grunted.

"Put on any brand you want. Just keep your eyes open and report, that's all." Nixon suddenly stepped close and his eyes narrowed and grew mean. "Ballard, you got any objections?"

"I don't know."

"Then don't look for 'em. Do the job—and live." He let the words sink in before he spoke again. "Might be that up there you'll see Hanes' daughter rather than him. That don't matter; she can hire too."

"Daughter?"

Nixon made a grimace. "A woman that'd make any man look twice. She and her father run the business like partners —like she could fill a man's shoes!" He walked to the door. "I'll not see you until after you're driving for Hanes. Get the job, Ballard, or you'll get a bullet. On the other hand, if you bring this off, you'll get a bonus. I can tell you that."

He lifted a finger, opened the door and was gone.

Ken looked at the blank panels of the closed door. Then he turned and studied the bills on the dresser, crisp and green and golden. Horse . . . saddle . . . gun . . . whip. Travel north and get a job with Hanes, who has a daughter.

He recalled the momentary glimpse he had had of the girl in the station yard. The daughter? Again came the stirring of the impulse to get another look at her. Ken angrily grabbed the money and shoved it in his pocket.

He caught his reflection in the wavery mirror and glared into his own angry eyes. "Don't you ever learn?" he demanded of himself, and then turned away.

On the evening of the fourth day, Ken rode easily into Sioux Springs. The jagged peaks of the Treachery Range now lined the southern horizon behind him. The town proved to be a small county seat, with the white-spired courthouse and church the two tallest buildings in town.

Ken's horse, a sleek bay, ambled across a bridge over a creek at the edge of the town, its hoofs sounding hollow on the wide thick boards. Approaching Ken came a big freight wagon, and he spurred the horse to leave the bridge before the wagon arrived. He pulled to one side and watched it pass.

It was a Hanes wagon, he knew, but there was no proud lettering such as Moran would use to mark it. Ken lightly spurred the bay on and entered the town. It had a single main business street, several blocks in length. The stores and buildings marked it as a supply center for a far-flung area about it.

Ken passed the Hanes station, not nearly as large as the one in Pass City. His eyes flicked in surprise when he read the words "Main Office" on the plainly lettered sign above the gates. He rode on, found a hotel, and his journey was over.

The next two days, following Nixon's instructions, Ken wandered about the town. He asked questions of the merchants about the ranches and towns in the area. There were three saloons in town, one of which, he learned, was frequented by Hanes' drivers and workers. He made it his saloon and by the second day had gained a nodding acquaintanceship with some of the customers.

The afternoon of the second day, he walked near the freight station. A light buggy wheeled out of the gates and rolled along the street toward him. A man drove, but a girl sat beside him. The girl caught Ken's attention. She was the same one he had seen back in Pass City. Now that he had a closer view, he saw she had fair glowing skin and eyes that, at this distance, looked either brown or deep violet. She wore a short jacket of dark material over a gray dress, whose flaring skirt swept down to her shoe tips. A pert bonnet sat on the bronze-red hair.

She looked toward Ken at that instant. Her eyes took him in and swept on. The carriage passed, the matched blacks moving smartly. Ken's impression of the man doing the driving was that he had dark, bold, handsome features, a hawklike nose, and a trim muscular body clothed in a dark suit.

Ken slowly moved on. So Hanes' daughter was here. Then he shrugged. What did it matter? Now he had had that second look and he could forget her.

That night, Ken again went to the saloon. He had a drink and then, on invitation, joined some men at a small-ante poker game. One he knew to be a Hanes foreman, Hal Smith. As the game progressed, the men became more friendly. The sheriff wandered in, and Ken looked up when the lawman stopped by the table. He spoke briefly to Smith, nodded to Ken, and then watched idly.

Ken lost the pot, threw in his cards and spoke casually to the foreman. "Hanes hiring?"

"Why? Do you know freighting?"

"Some. Outfit I was with went broke, so I wandered up this way. I like the feel of this country."

"I'll tell Lou about you. But I wouldn't gamble on a job, unless a new route opens. Lou's hands stay with him."

"No harm to ask. Always other jobs."

The sheriff said, "Lots of ranches around, if you're looking for a job."

Ken sighed. "Reckon I'll have to get a ranch job if I want to stay."

The batwings burst open and a wide-eyed, excited man looked over the crowd. He saw the lawman and rushed toward him. A sudden silence fell on the room.

"Sheriff, Lou Hanes wants you—fast. Three of his wagons were burned and a driver shot."

The lawman wheeled away and strode toward the doors. Over the room, chairs scraped and banged as men jumped up. Drinks and card games were forgotten as the crowd flowed through the batwings and out.

Ken followed the foreman onto the dark street. Down toward the freight station, he saw winking lanterns and the dark shapes of milling horses and men. He let the crowd take him forward till he found himself before the station gates.

The sheriff had disappeared into the office building, but Ken could see him and other men through the lighted windows. One of them was the man he had seen with the girl in the carriage. An older man briefly appeared and then moved beyond the angle of the window. Ken watched as the sheriff turned quickly. A moment later the lawman strode into the yard, with men behind him. Station employees had formed a curious and excited knot just within the yard.

The lawman's voice carried clearly to the street. "We're making up a posse—looks like outlaws have hit Sioux County again. Those willing to ride, go home and get your guns. Sparks, here, will issue rifles and Colts to any that don't have 'em. We leave in twenty minutes."

He strode through the gates, turned toward his office, then halted in midstride and faced the curious crowd on the walk. "Hunting outlaws is anybody's party. Any of you want to help, you're welcome."

He strode off. Several men in the crowd broke away and hurried up the street. Ken looked at the men within the gates, then at the office.

Tag Nixon, he knew with grim certainty, had given him the signal.

V

Ken went to his hotel room, closed the door and strode to the window without lighting the lamp. He looked down into the street, which was still stirring with excitement. He frowned, his strong fingers beating a tattoo on the window sill. Despite his inner certainty that Tag Nixon had pulled the attack on the wagons, there was no real proof.

Proof, Ken knew, could make a difference. He had believed, in the last few years, that nothing mattered, and he had allowed himself to sink deeper and deeper into a world without standards or meaning. Now he wasn't so sure. For someone to kill a man so Ken could get a job shocked him. He realized that all this time his real self had been slowly dying; worse, he himself had tried to kill it by a kind of slow strangulation.

He grinned without mirth, his eyes still bleak on the dark street below. Ironic that his kidnaping and training for this very job by a ruthless man like Brad Moran should have stirred old standards he had thought long since dead. Like a bum in heart and thought as well as in fact, he had drifted along. But now, he sensed, the time had come to make a decision. For that he needed proof.

He swung from the window and, still without

58

striking a light, opened one of the dresser drawers. Pulling out his gunbelt and holstered Colt, he quickly strapped the belt about his waist, his fingers checking the filled loops. Then he returned to the window and, by the half light, checked the Colt and the loads in the chambers. Finally he replaced the gun in the holster, turned and hurried from the room.

Not long after, he rode his saddled horse out of the livery stable and hurried along the street to the freight station. Gathered there were about thirty mounted men, Ken judged as he came up. He waited with the rest for the lawman, who came riding up a few moments later.

Ken raised his right hand with the others at the sheriff's grim order and repeated the deputy's oath. As they finished, a man came riding out of the station gates, and the lawman turned to him. "Ready to ride, Sparks?"

"In a minute. Lou's going along."

A second man rode out. Ken had a partial glimpse of a round, fleshy face, which he identified as that of the older man he had seen through the office window. Hanes swung his horse in beside the lawman, who lifted his arm as a signal and spurred his horse. Ken fell in with the rest as they rushed down the dark street and out of town.

The sheriff, Hanes and Sparks led the hard-riding posse. Ken peered ahead in the darkness but could make out few landmarks. The speed was too great, and the riders pressed too close about him. He felt the acrid sting of dust in his nostrils. The rolling thunder of many hoofs filled his ears.

Miles rolled back of them and then, far ahead, a spot of orange glowed in the night. The speed increased and soon Ken saw the orange spot was a big fire that guided them to the wagons. The spot grew larger, and then he noticed a low spread of glowing embers to one side of the fire —all that remained of a burned wagon.

The posse thundered up, pulled in with a swirl of dust that dulled the flames of the campfire for a moment. Then the dust rolled on and Ken saw men rising to meet the posse. He glimpsed a blanket-wrapped form lying to one side and his jaw momentarily set at a grim angle. He dismounted and strode to the fire with the other men.

Hanes might own the wagons, but his superintendent, Frank Sparks, took charge now. He shot questions at the drivers who stepped out to meet him. Ken looked at the high dark shapes of two other wagons just at the outer reach of light, and he heard horses snort. Then Sparks' harsh voice caught his attention.

"What's the damage? How did it happen?"

"One wagon burned, Frank," the driver replied. "Cargo lost. They tore up the goods in the other wagons and—"

Hanes cut in, "Who's hurt? That's important. How bad?"

"Jake Lacey," the driver answered. "Took a slug in the side. Lost a lot of blood before we could help him. He'll make it if we can get him to a doctor."

"Jake!" Hanes exclaimed. His voice tightened. "All right, get one of those wagons unloaded and hitched up."

He turned sharply and strode to the blanketed form. Now Ken had a clean look at him in the bright firelight. Hanes' round face showed deep concern as he bent over the wounded man. Some of the men hurried toward the wagons, but Sparks checked the driver he had questioned.

"How did it happen?"

Ken edged closer as the man replied. "They hit us just at dusk. We had pulled in here to camp but hadn't even unhitched. They rode in—about ten of 'em, I'd say. Came around the bend over there." He gestured into darkness beyond the fire. "Masked, every one. Jake made a move and took a slug."

Sparks' dark face looked hawk-angry but he said nothing as the driver continued. "I started to help Jake but the leader told me to stand hitched or take a bullet myself. There was nothing we could do, Frank, looking down the barrels of ten guns."

"All right!" Sparks snapped. "Go on."

61

"I guess Jake's move made them mad—leastways the leader. Like I said, they tore up the cargo. Acted like they thought we had payroll money hid somewhere. We didn't, of course."

The driver nodded toward the glowing embers. "The leader picked that wagon. Carried drygoods, kerosene and things like that for Everly's store. Went up like a torch, and we just had to stand there. Then they took the teams—every damn horse!—and rode off."

"How'd you get Ben started to town?"

"They turned the teams loose too soon, Frank. Not half an hour later, the first pair came ambling back. By then we had Jake patched up as good as we could. I figured it was best we stayed right here until the law came."

Sparks nodded, then whipped about. "Okay, let's ride."

The sheriff checked him. "Wait up, Frank."

"Wait up! What for? Every minute we stay here those outlaws get further away. I want every one of them in jail."

"So do I, Frank. But where you going to find 'em?"

Sparks stared, his face angrily flushed. He made a sweeping gesture beyond the fire. "We'll pick up their trail and—"

"How? In pitch dark?"

Sparks' head jerked up and his lips flattened.

"Ten riders would leave enough sign so a blind man could follow."

"Sure, at first. But after they cut loose the wagon teams, you can bet they started watching their tracks and leaving damn few. We'll camp until daybreak and—"

"No!" Sparks exploded. "We ride now!"

"Frank, maybe you'll ride and wear yourself out trying to find a trail. I won't."

"We'll see!" Sparks spun about.

The sheriff's grip on his arm checked him, and now the lawman's face had grown tight and harsh. "Get this, Frank. I'm sheriff and this is my posse. It follows my orders. So do you, so long as you wear that badge."

The eyes of the two men locked. Sparks finally threw off the restraining hand and grabbed at the deputy's badge. From the fire, Lou Hanes spoke sharply. "Frank! You're too mad to see that Harry's right. Calm down and let's get Jake on the way back to town. Daylight is soon enough to hunt outlaws."

Sparks stood frozen for a moment, his hand still on the badge. Then he took a deep breath, dropped his hand, turned on his heel and strode to the fire. The sheriff looked after him for a second and then, his face showing relief, ordered the possemen to picket their mounts.

Ken ground tied his horse and moved closer to the fire. Now Hanes and Sparks both bent over the wounded man, Hanes checking the bandaged side and looking worried. Sparks, still frowning, said something low. Hanes shook his head and Sparks slowly stood up.

The empty wagon had now been hitched and teamsters came to the fire. Under Hanes' directions they carefully lifted Jake and placed him in the wagonbed. Hanes delegated two of the men to ride with Jake, then signaled the driver. The wagon slowly moved out of the camp ground and disappeared into the night. For a few moments they could hear the noise of wheels and the clink of chains; then the sounds faded.

Hanes sighed and turned to the remaining teamsters clustered about him. "We can check the damage and straighten up the cargo."

They moved out. Ken watched Sparks stride angrily away. Hanes walked to the sheriff, who stood near Ken. The freighter looked after Sparks for a moment as he organized the work; then Hanes spoke softly. "Harry, he's mad and not thinking. He'll be all right after a while."

"I know. I won't hold it against him. He's a good man."

"Too quick with the temper at times." Hanes shrugged. "But that's needed sometimes."

Hanes moved out to help with the work. Ken stood near the fire among the others—men who did not work for Hanes. In his own way, he was as anxious as Sparks to move out and find the outlaw trail. It might confirm his suspicion as to who had led the attack, and why. A muscle jumped slightly in his jaw as he considered the role he was to play—a spy for Brad Moran.

His attention swung to the workers as he heard Sparks' voice lifted in swift, incisive orders. He was a hard and driving man, Ken knew, undoubtedly completely loyal to Lou Hanes. The line's troubleshooter, Ken recalled, and certainly fitted for the job, now that Ken saw him in action.

The teamsters were working at stacking the unloaded cargo, Sparks and Hanes laboring with the men. There were pitifully few of them, Ken saw, and he glanced at the possemen about him. He moved out from the fire and started to help with the work. A teamster gave him a surprised but grateful look as Ken bent to help with a heavy box. They moved it to the growing pile and straightened.

Suddenly Sparks stood before Ken, dark brows drawn in angry puzzlement. "Who are you?"

Ken gestured toward the fire. "I came with the posse. Looks like you need some extra hands here."

Lou Hanes had come up behind Sparks as the man snapped, "We need know-how as well as muscles."

"Nothing to lifting and stacking," Ken said.

"It's to be loaded, if possible, in one wagon."

"I've done a lot of that."

Hanes spoke up. "You're a teamster?"

Ken hesitated, realizing he had moved too fast because of his urge to help. But he could not back away now. "That's right."

"I've not seen you around before," Sparks snapped.

"That figures. I been in Sioux Springs just a few days."

"Drifter!" Sparks snorted, and shook his head. "We can do without that kind."

"Wait, Frank," Hanes remonstrated. "Let him help. That doesn't mean he's on the payroll. We can use a pair of experienced hands."

Sparks made an irritable gesture. "Okay, Lou. Seems like it's my night to tangle up."

He stalked away. Hanes looked worriedly after him for a moment and then nodded to Ken. "Pitch in. I'll settle later for what we'll owe you."

"Nothing. Who gets paid to help somebody in trouble?" Ken said shortly.

He turned to the work and Hanes, after a second's hesitation, hurried after Sparks. Ken pitched in and, within a short time, the remaining wagon had been reloaded, the excess cargo stacked and covered with a tarp. Sparks assigned three of his men to guard it until other wagons could be sent out from town.

The work done, the Hanes men wearily rejoined the posse. Hanes, Sparks, and the sheriff conferred over the amount of goods destroyed in the fire and Ken, sprawled some distance away, watched them.

He knew that his helpful impulse had brought him to Hanes' attention, but he hadn't wanted to do that until he had made up his own mind. He could still see Jake Lacey's blanketed form—a man cold-bloodedly eliminated to make a job for Ken. He growled deep in his throat and jerked around to face the fire.

The dark hours dragged by but at last the eastern sky lightened. The men stirred, moving stiffened muscles and joints. Sparks was the first up and out of his blankets. He rolled them, hurried to his horse and was ready to go by the time the possemen moved, yawning to the fire. Someone put on a coffee pot.

Sparks called, "That can wait. The outlaws won't."

The sheriff answered patiently. "They will be worn out by now; they've ridden all night. Get some hot brew in your blood, Frank. The day won't seem half so hard and long."

The superintendent cursed under his breath, wheeled his horse and rode off. The sheriff turned to the fire with a patient shrug. In a unhurried voice, he set the men to checking their guns and horses while the coffee brewed. When it had boiled, the men returned to the fire. They had only to gulp down the hot brew and mount.

Ken had just finished his mug when Sparks

came pounding back. He swung out of saddle and strode up to the sheriff. "While you've been killing time, I found their trail. They cut loose the teams to blot it and then changed directions. They headed south."

The sheriff nodded. "I figured they'd cut back. Okay, boys, let's find us some bandits."

They mounted and rode out. Ken was in the forefront of the posse, not far behind the sheriff, Sparks, and Hanes. They followed a broad trail of many hoofs and then came to the place where the teams had been abandoned. Sparks merely indicated sign with a flip of the hand and rode off to the right along a lesser trail.

It made a wide circle and cut south and east. Ken sighted along the direction of the trail and saw the distant, hazy peaks of the Treacheries. Once the outlaws hit those mountains, he knew, they'd have a maze of canyons and draws in which to lose themselves.

The sheriff set a fast pace, but it did not please Sparks. He kept pushing ahead, obviously impatient to get the quarry in sight. The sun mounted higher, and still the trail lay plain before them. Ken saw that it headed like an arrow toward the mountains, now looming slightly higher against the sky.

They came on a series of low hills and had to thread their way between them. Still they followed plain sign, and now Ken sharply judged the distance to the mountains. The outlaws could not reach that haven until late in the day, unless they about killed their mounts, and that was too much of a risk. Ken wondered if the outlaws had some other hideout.

The sign worked along the shallow draws and dips between the hills, then suddenly broke free. Ahead was rolling grazing land that seemed to sweep on and on to the distant mountains. Far off to the left Ken saw the black shapes of grazing cattle. The outlaws' trail veered in that direction.

Up ahead, Sparks suddenly drew rein as Hanes and the sheriff rode up. A few moments later, Ken and the posse formed a waiting half circle behind the three leaders.

Ken watched Sparks cut back and forth, while the lawman quartered about far to his right. The two men met and conferred, Sparks with angry gestures while the sheriff shook his head. Ken moved out from the group, slowly walking his horse, eyes to the ground. Within a matter of minutes he knew what had happened. The sign was clear.

The outlaws had drifted into the herd and, for a time, tracks of steer and horse were clearly separate. Then the beef had been stampeded. A gun shot, the crack of a lariat against leather chaps, a shout—the beef had raced south and east, the riders among them. After that the ground was too churned up to show any clear sign.

Ken looked up to find the sheriff's knowing eye on him. Hanes now talked intently to Sparks, who took the low-toned orders with ill grace. Ken drifted along the churned ground where the stampede had been. He drew rein, seeing where a single rider had cut away. Then he moved on, soon came on sign of another rider cutting from the racing herd. This man had taken a different direction from the first.

Ken neck reined his horse around and moved back to the posse. Sparks, his handsome face sullen, sat stiff and straight in the saddle. As Ken moved closer, the sheriff called, "Well?"

Ken turned toward him. Sparks and Hanes watched him closely. Ken shrugged. "They used an old Indian trick, except they used the beef to mess up sign even worse than usual. They scattered in every direction, each man for himself."

The sheriff turned in triumph to Sparks. "There you are, Frank. It's what I said."

"We can still ride 'em down—follow one until he joins up with the rest again."

Ken shook his head. "Too easy, and this bunch knows it. Leastways, their leader does. Sioux Springs is close, and who'd notice single riders there?"

Hanes said, "He's right, Frank."

Sparks shot a baffled, angry look at Ken, then

at the sheriff. "You're taking the word of a range drifter—"

"Hold up!" the lawman snapped as Ken jerked erect in his saddle. "You're throwing your weight, Frank. He read sign just as I did, but you're too mad to see it."

"Then we're just giving up right here?"

"We'll follow one trail," the lawman conceded. "But I know what will happen."

He moved out, eyes to the ground. Soon he lifted his arm in a signal for the posse to follow and struck out along the prints left by a single rider. They moved almost due east, toward the hills that curved southward. The trail led them into a narrow swale, threaded the hills and then abruptly changed course. The posse followed sign in a huge curve that took them west again finally and struck the main road far south of where the attack on the wagons had occurred. There sign vanished.

The sheriff drew rein and looked at Sparks. The superintendent's tight face acknowledged defeat. He made a resigned gesture. "All right, Harry—you called it. What now?"

"Back to town and hope we get some line. We're wasting time out here."

Sparks fell in with the riders as the sheriff turned toward Sioux Springs. The excitement gone and defeat riding them, the posse fell silent. In a short time the town was ahead, and soon they were riding empty handed down the main street. The sheriff drew rein before the freighting station. The girl Ken had seen twice before ran out but the excitement died in her eyes as she read the news in the attitude of the riders. She watched silently as the sheriff dismissed the men with his wry thanks. Ken eyed the girl, again struck by her beauty. When the sheriff had finished, Ken lifted the reins to turn with the others.

Hanes checked him. "You've freighted, you said."

Ken saw that the girl's attention turned to him and that Sparks also watched with a strange hard glint in his eyes. Ken nodded cautiously. "Some."

"Where?"

"Oh—south. I come from New Mexico."

Hanes studied him, said suddenly, "Want to work for me?"

Ken hesitated. Here was the job he had been told to get and he had only to agree. But he still could not be sure that he would go along with Moran's plan. He moistened his lips. "Let me think it over."

Hanes' face fell. "All right. But let me know by afternoon. I need a driver."

He turned away. Sparks, with a look of pleased relief, fell in with him and they rode through the station gate as the girl turned back to the office.

Ken stabled the horse and then walked slowly

back to the hotel. Afternoon, he thought, the time of decision. So far, he had drifted along with events, glad to escape the hobo jungle, to have money in his pocket, to feel that he had at least been lifted a cut above the drifting bum. But he could not be sure he wanted to go along any further with Moran.

True, Moran had said there'd be no gunplay or killing for him to do. But if Moran had planned this raid and ordered Nixon to pull it off, what dependence could there be in his promise? Ken scented violence, and he wanted no part of it. He almost turned on his heel and walked back to the stable with the thought of saddling up again and riding out, but an inherent caution checked him. Make sure, he told himself.

He entered the hotel, mounted the stairs and walked down the hall to his room. He sailed his hat onto the bed, unbuckled his gunbelt, walked to the window and looked down on the street. It seemed empty and peaceful. Let it stay that way, he thought.

A light tap on the door brought him around. He opened it and looked at Tag Nixon's heavy, inscrutable face. Nixon walked in unconcernedly when Ken stepped aside. Ken searched for signs of hard riding or a sleepless night, but found none.

Nixon dropped into the chair, cuffed his hat back on his head. "Never figured you to be a law-abiding sort of man. And here you been riding all night with the sheriff!"

Ken remained by the door. "What do you know about it?"

"Saw you ride in."

"About the raid on the wagons?" Ken snapped.

"Oh, that. Heard talk. Saw 'em bring a man in. Shot up pretty bad, I heard."

"You don't know?"

Nixon smiled. "I don't worry about what happens to Hanes. But I do know he lost a driver. He needs one."

Ken moved slowly into the room. "Nixon, you raided those wagons."

The man's face tightened. "I was right here in town, and I got proof of it."

"Your men?"

Nixon shrugged. "One witness is as good as another. Now . . . when are you going to hit Hanes for a job?"

"I don't have to. He's already asked me."

"Well, now! That was easy."

"I didn't take it."

Nixon stared and his brows slowly drew down. "Why not?"

Ken moved to the window, looked out a moment and then turned to face the gunman. "In three years I sank pretty low and did some things I'm not proud of. Begging, sodden drunk on cheap wine, cutting corners to keep alive, stealing a shirt off a clothesline—but nothing that hurt anyone more'n I hurt myself."

Nixon sat unmoving, eyes steady, but there was a subtle threat about the bulk of him. Ken sensed it, faltered for a moment and then took a grip on his determination.

"I have to thank you and Moran for taking me out of that life. I owe you for that. But now I'm not sure where you're driving me. I think you raided those wagons. I think you deliberately shot Jake Lacey so I could take his job. I think you didn't give a damn whether your bullet wounded or killed him. If that's true, then what do you plan for Hanes?"

Nixon growled, "Ballard, you're just supposed to do what you're told."

Ken took a deep breath. "Oh, no! There's a big-trouble smell about this. I've gone along, figuring I owed Moran something. I'm willing to pay. But I've got a hunch that just driving and telling you about Hanes' business isn't the end of it."

Nixon stood up and his hand moved slowly along the leather of his holster. Ken felt his muscles tighten, but Nixon did not touch the protruding handle of the Colt. Finally, the big hand dropped away and Nixon walked to the door, turned there to face Ken again.

"I told you once, Moran always gets his money's worth. He took you over, headed you for Hanes. What he plans after that is his business. But you figure how much he'll depend on a bum like you to do something important."

Ken's eyes blazed, but Nixon bored on in his heavy tight voice. "So you get to Hanes and you take that job. You follow orders. That's one way to pay Brad back. He expects it."

It sounded reasonable, but Ken was not entirely convinced. His uncertainty showed in his eyes, and Nixon's face suddenly hardened. His hand dropped to his holster. "How many men hit those wagons last night?"

Ken showed his surprise at the question. "Ten."

"Now where do you reckon they are? And who they are? How you reckon to avoid a bullet day or night that might come from any of ten directions?" Nixon's lips curled in an ugly smile. "As I said, Moran gets his money's worth—one way or another. By nightfall, you'd better be on Hanes' payroll."

He nodded, a curt bob of the head, opened the door and moved out in the hall. The door closed softly behind him, leaving Ken to stare at the blank, indifferent panels.

VI

The afternoon shadows were stretching long in the street when Ken approached the freighting station. There had been no sign of Tag Nixon from the moment he had walked out of the hotel room, but Ken knew that meant nothing. His threat still stood, and any of nine unknown men could execute it. They would bide their time until nightfall. Until then, they would watch, any or all of them.

The open gate of the station stood just ahead. Ken's steps slowed and he looked back down the street. It looked normal and peaceful, but any one of the men loafing on the saloon porch or walking along the street could be working for Brad Moran. Ken's life or death could hinge on the next few moments. To turn around and walk away from the job would mark him for a bullet tonight or tomorrow. It could come from the darkness between buildings, out of the mouth of an alley, in his hotel room—or along a road, if he tried to leave the town. Nixon had made no empty threat. Jake Lacey was proof of that.

Ken moved reluctantly toward the gates. He had no choice, if he wanted to live. It was one thing to challenge a man and meet a showdown face to face. It was another to have no chance, to know lead could smash into his back without warning. He growled under his breath, cursing himself for a situation not entirely his fault. He walked through the gates.

The office he entered was furnished much like Brad Moran's, back in Pass City. But there the similarity ended. As he entered, Frank Sparks half turned from the rail barrier. Beyond it sat Lou Hanes, round face troubled. His daughter looked up from a desk by the window.

Sparks' dark eyes flashed when he saw Ken. "What do you want?"

Lou Hanes' round face flooded with pleased surprise and his plump hand made a swift gesture toward Sparks. "I asked him to come in, Frank."

"The drifter!"

Ken flushed, but Hanes cut in quickly, "Maybe, Frank. But maybe a good hand with a wagon and teams."

"I doubt it," Frank snapped, and turned to the door. Ken moved slightly to one side to let the man by and he read dislike on the handsome face. Sparks left, the door banging noisily behind him.

Hanes said, "All of us are touchy, what with the raid and Jake being shot. Frank'll get over it."

Ken nodded and came to the barrier. He was too much aware of the girl at the far desk, though he didn't look directly at her. But the musty office held a subtle fragrance, and now and then he heard the rustle of her long, flaring skirt or the sound of her pen.

Hanes gestured Ken inside, where he took a chair beside the man's small desk. Hanes looked hopefully at him. "You said you'd freighted—in New Mexico, wasn't it?"

Ken hesitated a fraction of a second, but then his eyes cut to the window looking out on the street. On the far walk he saw a man leaning against the corner of a building. The man's hatbrim hid the upper portion of his face, but late sun glinted on the bright cartridges in the loops of his gunbelt.

"That's right."

"You rode with us," Hanes said, "so you know we lost a driver—for a long time, anyway. So we need a man. But I'd like someone with experience."

"I've got it," Ken said truthfully.

Hanes rubbed his hand along his jaw. His eyes sharpened. "But a long way from here. What brought you up to this part of the country?"

"Change of scenery. I worked desert country."

The girl's voice came suddenly, clear and musical. "Do you know Brad Moran?"

"I've met him," Ken said shortly, and added with sincere bitterness, "From what I've seen and heard, I don't like his methods."

The girl and her father exchanged glances. Ken looked up to catch the dark violet eyes weighing him. They held a moment and he felt the impact of her beauty, noted the grave set of the soft lips. A slight color came to her cheeks and she hastily looked away.

Hanes stirred and Ken's eyes swung back to him. "Who'd you work for down in New Mexico?"

Ken heard the yard door open behind him as he answered, "Hauled for myself."

A heavy step sounded and then Sparks looked down from the other side of the railing. "What kind of experience is that? You're just cadging for a job—any job that'll bring a buck or two until you drift on."

"Now, Frank, I'm not so sure—" Lou started, but Sparks' sardonic expression stopped him.

"Lou, there are a dozen town men we can get. Maybe they don't have the *experience* of this one, but at least we know something about them. They're not drifting bums."

"Frank, you're unfair!" The girl spoke sharply.

He swung to face her. "Alice, I can judge a man, and I know what I'm doing."

Ken heard the rustle of her skirt, then her light step. "We need someone in Jake's place, right away. If this man can handle horses and a wagon, as he says, then we'd be foolish to break in a green hand. I say be fair and at least give him a chance to prove himself."

She now stood beside the desk, facing Sparks. Ken saw the lift of her head, the angry set of the delicately molded chin. The soft gray material of her dress curved smoothly over full breasts, accented now by her angry breathing.

Ken suddenly realized that Sparks watched him, dark eyes narrowed and glinting. The man's look slanted to Alice Hanes, then back to Ken. "Come out in the yard."

"Frank," the girl asked sharply, "what are you going to do?"

"See if he's a driver, or if he's what I think he is. That's about as fair as you can be—unless someone has objections."

He smiled crookedly. Ken stood up, moved around Alice to the swing gate. "That's fair enough for me."

Sparks wheeled about and led the way to the yard. Lou and Alice followed, waited by the door as Sparks strode across the yard and halted before a big empty wagon against the far wall. He indicated it and then the stable.

"There's a wagon. Horses are in the stable. There's a load on the dock. Let me see you put 'em together."

Ken nodded, turned to the stable. Sparks followed slowly after him, certain that he'd show up the drifter. He nodded assent to the hostlers when Ken asked which teams would be used, and they indicated four heavy animals.

Ken worked smoothly, placing the harness on two of the animals. He led them out and up to the wagon, attached the team to the trees. He returned to the stable and soon reappeared with the lead team. They were as quickly hitched to the wagon.

He climbed into the high seat, picked up the lines. Easily backing the wagon to the loading dock, he was aware that Alice watched him with growing approval, though Sparks' expression revealed angry surprise. Hal Smith, the foreman Ken had met at the saloon, looked on in blank puzzlement.

As Ken swung out of the high seat, Sparks jumped agilely up on the dock. Lou Hanes had crossed the yard and stood nearby as Sparks indicated a stack of crates, barrels, and boxes. "There's the load."

Ken asked, "Where are the manifests? Do you know the route?"

"Just let me see you load," Sparks snapped.

Ken calmly faced him. "A drifter might do just that. But he'd not know his business. Last delivery goes in first—first delivery at the gate, where it should be."

"He's freighted," Lou said in satisfaction.

Sparks' jaw set stubbornly. "We'll still see. Load the wagon."

It was hard work, but finally it was done. At the end, freight filled the wagon and Ken threw the heavy canvas over the load and lashed it tight. Alice had returned to the office long before, but

Lou Hanes remained. He looked with approval on the finished job, then turned to his foreman.

"Well, Frank?"

Sparks shrugged. "Hire him if you want."

"I want. Ballard, you're on the payroll as of now. Run the wagon over to the wall and stable the teams. You're already loaded for your first run in the morning. Come to the office and I'll show you the route on the map."

Ken nodded, jumped off the dock. In a few moments he led the horses back into the stable and removed the harness. The hostlers led them to their stalls and Ken started across the yard to the office.

Sparks hailed him from the loading dock. When Ken halted in the yard just below him, Sparks looked impassively down on him for a long moment. Finally he broke the silence.

"Lou's hired you, Ballard. But I'm the one who keeps the wagons rolling. Don't make a mistake."

He turned sharply away. Ken remained standing, looking after him. He couldn't quite understand Sparks' antagonism, except that the man resented Ken's part in the futile pursuit of the wagontrain raiders. Ken shoved his hands in his pockets and turned slowly toward the office. He had taken this job under Nixon's threat and he had felt trapped from the moment he walked into the office. Now Sparks' plain dislike added to the complications. Work here would not be easy. But what would it be like if Sparks, or any of them, discovered he had been placed here by Brad Moran? He pushed that thought aside.

In the office, Lou Hanes showed him the route he would follow—northward to several small outlying cowtowns and a couple of big ranches. Then Lou turned him over to his daughter. She signaled him to take the seat beside her desk.

He sat down on the edge of the chair, nervously turning his bat in his hands. This girl had too much of an effect on him. Her nearness tended to confuse him and, because of it, he felt an irritation both at her and at himself.

She had given him but a swift glance as she indicated the chair. Now she kept her eyes on her paper and pen as she listed his name, asked where he lived. She looked up when he mentioned the hotel.

"Will you stay there?" She flushed when she met his puzzled stare. "I mean, a driver's wages are not exactly high."

"Sure, but I was just riding through."

"There are rooms or shacks around town to be had. Of course, it's none of my business."

"I'll look for one when I come back from this run. Know of any?"

"Perhaps we can help," she answered stiffly. "We'll see how it works out. Now, are you married?"

"No, ma'am."

He said it so sharply that she looked up again.

She seemed about to ask a question, choked it back. She noted the information, nodded and then said, "Payday's almost a month off. Will you need an advance?"

"No, ma'am. I can get by."

Only then did she look up and fully meet his eyes. She smiled, friendly and warm. "Now you work for us, Mr. Ballard. I'm sure we'll all get along."

"So am I," he blurted and then jerked to his feet to cover his confusion. He looked down at her. "Thank you, ma'am."

Lou spoke from his desk. "We're thankful you came along at the right time. We'd sure be in a bind, with Lacey knocked out for maybe weeks or months."

He stood up and Ken shook hands. Then Ken bobbed his head at Alice and fled from the office. Sparks was not in sight when he stepped into the yard. The warehouse foreman signaled him over to the dock.

"You on the payroll?" he asked, squatting at the edge of the dock. When Ken nodded, he looked over and beyond him toward the stable. "Give you a tip, then. Look out and walk sharp if Frank's in sight. He don't like you."

"I don't know why. I've done him no harm."

"No, but I figure Frank thinks you showed him up in front of the sheriff and Lou Hanes when you were out with the posse. He was mad, and he gets stubborn then. Good man, Frank, but he don't like to be crossed. He'll get over it in time if you sort of walk wide around him."

"Thanks. But why are you telling me?"

The foreman grinned and straightened. "You and me have played poker together. If you hold this job, I might get some of that money back."

Ken grinned, then sobered. "I'll try to walk wide and speak soft—for a time. But I figure a reasonable man don't hold a mad too long."

"Frank won't; you'll see."

The foreman nodded, stood up and walked away into the depths of the warehouse. Ken turned and walked toward the gates and the street. As he passed the office, he glanced in. Lou and Alice Hanes sat at their desks, the girl half turned about, talking to her father.

Ken's step slowed. Hanes, he thought, was a warm and friendly man. His daughter was disturbing and pretty. Probably all their money was tied up in this freighting business, and it also represented years of effort and building. And Ken had been placed here to wreck it, in some way unknown to him.

He bit his lip, wanting to step into the office and tell them both he didn't want their job. But then what would happen to Ken Ballard? He felt trapped. Suddenly he sensed that someone was watching. He looked back and saw Frank Sparks on the warehouse dock. The superintendent stood quite still and yet somehow looked tense with anger. Ken hurried on through the gates and turned into the street.

When he entered the dusty lobby of the hotel, a stranger looked up at him from one of the cracked leather chairs. The man was small and wiry, with a dark, pinched face. A black stubble of beard covered emaciated jowls. Ken gave him a single glance, taking in the cartridge belt and holstered gun. Then he started across the lobby.

The stranger stood up. "Ballard?"

Ken stopped short and swung around. The stranger hitched at his belt. "Friend of yours sent me."

"Who are you?"

"Hank Scatlin, if that means anything to you. Point is, we both got a friend in Pass City. He's worried about you some. Wondered if you got that job you needed."

Ken's blue eyes were level and frosty. Then he sighed, fully aware now that any idea he'd had of refusing Nixon or riding out was doomed.

"I got the job."

"Sure?"

Ken's eyes flashed. "You can watch me roll a wagon out in the morning."

Scatlin pursed thin lips. "Someone just might do that, Ballard. Your friend sure thinks a heap about you."

He made a careless, easy gesture and strolled out the open door to the street.

VII

At dawn the next morning, Ken pushed a bedroll under the high seat of the freight wagon, while the hostlers brought out the four horses and hitched them. He checked with the foreman, picked up the manifests. Other wagons stood at the dock and the big building was a bedlam of noise. The foreman wished him luck and hurried away to supervise the assembly of another cargo.

Ken walked to his wagon, throwing a glance at the closed office door across the yard. He could see Lou inside, talking to some drivers, but Alice was not in sight. Ken climbed onto the seat, gathered the reins and, with a slap of leather and a few quiet words to the horses, started across the yard.

He rolled into the street, making a wide circle on the turn, and then headed north. As he straightened out he saw Hank Scatlin leaning against a building, thumbs hooked into his gunbelt. Scatlin watched impassively as Ken passed, making no sign. Ken glanced back and saw the man pull his shoulders from the wall and stroll casually away.

Ken's lips set. Tag Nixon would know very soon that his puppet had moved as the strings were pulled. Ken grunted angrily and slapped the reins, voice lifting to the horses. The buildings wheeled by, were soon replaced by houses that gradually grew more scattered, and then he rolled out on the open range, the road dusty and yellow before him.

His way lay northward, at first across pleasant, rolling range country. He settled to the long monotonous grind, pulling his hatbrim down against the bright rising sun. Night found him many miles out and he rolled off the road under a grove of trees.

Within a short time the horses had been unharnessed and staked out to graze and rest. Ken's fire made a pleasant red glow against the gathering shadows as the coffee pot bubbled and the bacon and beans made savory odors. His bedroll lay to one side, ready for use.

By dawn he was up and on the move again. The first day set the pattern for all the rest as he worked northward, unloading bits of his cargo at crossroads stores, cowtown emporiums, saloons, and twice at big syndicate ranches. Men looked curiously at him at those places, but he did not have to explain about Jake Lacey. In the mysterious way of the range, the news had sped before him.

Late in the afternoon of the fifth day, he rolled down the short street of the cowtown that would mark the farthest reach of his run. Hanes had a small station here, including a smithy, a warehouse, and a few wagons for transshipments further north. Ahead, looming over the town, Ken saw the high jagged peaks of another mountain range, still bright with sun while the town filled with purple shadows.

Lamps came on in the stores and when Ken swung the nearly empty wagon into the station, he saw the glow of light in the office. He reined in and started to move off the seat but stopped short in surprise as the door opened and Frank Sparks came out.

The superintendent came out in the yard, followed by a balding, chunky man who was obviously the manager. Ken recovered from his surprise and dropped to the ground as Sparks came up.

"Well, you kept your schedule," he said, a touch grudgingly. "Any trouble—or sign of it?"

"Nothing." Ken handed his manifests and receipts to the manager and then added to Sparks, "I didn't expect to see you up here. No sign of you along the road."

"I work that way, Ballard. Surprise. Keeps the men on their toes. You can expect it."

He turned away without another word. The bald manager looked sharply at Ken. "You'll be loaded out for the return in the morning, Ballard. Fresh teams and a different wagon. First thing."

"Do I camp here tonight?"

"Lou keeps a room at the hotel for our drivers. He pays for it." He half turned, then stopped. "Saloon's next door. Just don't lap up too much rotgut."

"What makes you think I will? Or have you been listening to someone?"

"Just telling you, like I would any new man. See you in the morning."

The hotel proved to be typical of the cowtowns, a high and narrow box of a building, the rooms barely furnished with bed, dresser and chair. But it was clean enough and welcome after the long drive. After a bath and a shave, Ken found a small café across the street. He ate with relish, glad to escape from the road fare of bacon, beans and doughy biscuits.

It was full night when he came out on the street. Most of the stores had closed and the street was dark except for lights from the café behind him, the livery down the street, the hotel and saloon across the way before him. A few horses stood at the rack and Ken recalled the warning of the station manager.

He checked back irritation. The man's suspicions had obviously come from Sparks. Still, a small need to revolt rode Ken and, defiantly, he crossed the street and entered. The saloon was a small place, with a few tables and a bar at the far end of the room. A card game progressed at the only occupied table and half a dozen men stood at the bar. One of them was Sparks.

He glanced toward the batwings as Ken entered, and his dark eyes narrowed. He watched Ken approach, then swung away and tossed down the drink before him. Ken ordered a whiskey, caught Sparks' sharp eyes in the mirror and pleasantly nodded. The superintendent made a scant motion with his head.

Ken savored the bite of the whiskey, its warm explosion in his stomach. He looked at the empty shot glass and remembered that there had been a time but a few months ago when he had desperately sought the numbing stupor that liquor brought, and he'd have given his soul for a shot of rotgut. Now he drank from pleasure, not need. Give Moran credit, he thought ironically. Strange how something good could come out of something he sensed was basically evil.

Thought of Moran and his present job made him look at Sparks' reflection. He caught the man's suspicious eyes directly on him, weighing and probing.

Sparks suddenly moved over to Ken, indicated his glass. Ken shook his head. "I got orders against too much drinking."

"They still go," Sparks answered curtly. "But one more won't hurt. That's also an order."

Ken shrugged and watched the glass being refilled. He lifted it in a slight salute to Sparks, took a swallow and then asked, "Why?"

"One way of starting a talk. You've rubbed me the wrong way since I first laid eyes on you, Ballard. I want to know why."

"Well! That's playing all the cards face up."

"I like it that way. Always have." Sparks eyed Ken narrowly. "What brought you to Sioux Springs?"

"I told you—and Hanes."

"Sure, but I don't have to believe it."

Ken held his voice even. "Suit yourself."

Sparks studied him for a second longer; then his eyes moved down to his half-filled glass. "I admit you can handle horses and wagons. Nothing I can find wrong with your work."

Ken answered with a touch of acid, "Maybe it's my blue eyes."

Surprisingly, Sparks nodded. "That's part of it. They keep roaming where they're not supposed to be."

"Now what does that mean?"

"Back at the main station—Alice Hanes."

"Her!" Ken stared at Sparks, who didn't look around. But his nostrils had grown pinched and his jaw was thrust slightly forward. "I guess I didn't hear you and she are married . . . or engaged . . . or something like that."

"Not married, not engaged. But we're pretty close."

"And you think I—"

"You just keep your distance with her."

Ken chuckled without mirth. "Now I'll show some cards. Miss Hanes is a woman a man can't help seeing—you know that. So I've looked. But I'm not about to tangle up with any woman, let alone one another man wants."

Sparks looked around then and Ken saw the suspicion and disbelief still in his eyes. Ken shook his head. "You can bank on it. I'll have to look at her and talk to her. I'll be polite and friendly. But nothing beyond that."

"Let's say I'll believe you as far as I can see you."

Ken pushed away from the bar, hands braced against it. "Sparks, a pretty woman stripped me down to nothing not long ago. Oh, she didn't steal or take anything like money. But she stole every hope I ever had, every plan. She tore up something inside that made me tick."

Sparks openly stared now. Ken's blue eyes grew bitter, then cleared. "So I'm not about to lose it all over again. That puts my cards face up, I guess."

He turned then and strode to the batwings and out onto the dark porch of the saloon. He took a deep breath, exhaled it with a shuddering sigh. By an effort of will he pushed the memories away, squared his shoulders and walked the short distance to his hotel.

The memories stayed away until he had undressed and stretched out on the bed. They began to press in then and he tried to drown them in sleep. But that would not come and he lay wide awake, looking up into the darkness toward the low ceiling that was a lighter colored blur above him.

The pictures began to form. He saw the low,

94

warm adobe houses and false-fronted stores of the New Mexico town, the pastel shadings of the mesas and low mountains above and beyond it. He saw the rushing little stream, sun dappled from the willows, where he had first met Carla Wayne.

Carla! Great, dark, inviting eyes came vividly to his memory, and the full red lips that could grow so soft and wanton under his own. He could feel her again in his arms, could almost hear her voice.

The sheer pain of the memories shook him fully awake and he sat up, his face bleak in the darkness. But he had admitted Carla and the other memories came now. As they flooded in he lived over again the sweetness, ecstasy, and torture of what had once been his life.

He again sat in the bank long ago and signed a mortgage on a small spread he had bought for Carla and himself. Every cent he had saved or could borrow had gone into it and the few head of cattle that eventually would make him the big rancher she wanted him to be.

He could see her in her father's store, throwing him a secretive, meaningful look as she waited on a customer . . . the box suppers at the church, when she signaled which box was hers so that he could bid it in . . . the stolen moments by the creek just beyond her house.

These were the sweet remainders of the past, the glowing hopes and dreams. He made a grimace in the darkness of the cramped hotel room. He had not seen the little signs that should have warned him. Too much in love, he had been blind to the hard, shrewd core within Carla Wayne. He should have noticed. It showed clearly in her disdain of men in town and on the range who worked for others; in the way she pushed him beyond his financial abilities so he would own a spread. She made it clear she would only marry a rancher with a future, never a puncher.

Hindsight—how clear it is! His jaw clamped as the later memories crowded in. It had been wonderful at first. Carla was not one to hold back favors. Eyes, kisses, body, all had spun a web of blindness about him. He could see it now, but then he had moved in a world built solely around her. Blind fool! Had he thought, he would have realized that Ken Ballard was the only young and unmarried rancher in the area. Carla conferred her passion with an eye to the future return, instead of with love for the sake of the beloved. The ranch, small as it was, had been the one thing that held Carla to him. But he hadn't known that then. He had fatuously thought it was himself alone.

He recalled the day the news had come that a syndicate outfit had bought three of the ranches south of town. Like everyone else, Ken could talk only of that. So did Carla—and he had not fully recognized the hunger and envy in her voice. A month later a stranger appeared in town—young, assured, son of the principal stockholder of the syndicate.

That had marked the change, the rending of the dream. Ken had pressed Carla for a formal engagement and she had agreed to consider it. But, she said, he had only just started his new spread and it would be best to see how it would work. Her kiss had killed all of his arguments and made the whole thing sound reasonable. Ken threw himself into ranch work with more intensity than ever.

The strange young face—Chad Rayburn's— began to appear more and more about the town. Ken met him at the saloon, in the stores. Then he appeared at the box supper at the church, and somehow drew Carla's box . . . and took her home. The next day Carla explained that Ken must have missed her signal. She had to be polite to Mr. Rayburn; after all, his ranch had become very important to her father's store. How could she simply walk away from him? Surely, Ken could see the whole incident meant nothing.

So he tried to tell himself she was right, and he almost succeeded. But not quite. Even so, he had not been prepared when the blow fell. He had ridden in one Saturday, gone directly to the store. Carla was not there and her father had been strangely embarrassed and evasive. Puzzled, Ken had gone to her home. No one answered his knock, though he was certain she was there.

He had worriedly gone back to the small business district, bought some supplies, and then gone to the saloon. It was filled as usual on Saturdays, but there was a strangely festive air in the group about Chad Rayburn at the bar.

Ken had caught part of it as he pushed through the batwings and started across the crowded room. A sudden silence fell and he felt probing, uncertain eyes on him. Chad Rayburn had turned and the laughter died on his lips. He made a move as though to leave, then checked himself. This strange, tense atmosphere, Ken sensed, had something to do with him.

Rayburn eased back against the bar but his handsome face was tight, uncertain. He signaled the bartender. "A drink for Mr. Ballard."

Ken nodded puzzled thanks, lifted the glass in a gesture to Rayburn. "Your health and luck."

Rayburn's breath nearly whistled out in a deep sigh of relief. "Then you don't hold a grudge against me?"

"Grudge? What for?"

Rayburn stared. "You don't know? You haven't seen Carla?"

"No, not yet. But what—"

"My God!" Rayburn blurted. He whipped about and almost ran through the batwings. They swung crazily behind him as Ken stared, drink still poised in his hand.

He looked blankly around. "What kind of a burr's under his saddle?"

The bartender stood well back against the rear shelves. He spoke with difficulty. "Ken, we thought you knew. Hadn't seen you around town for over a week."

"I was fencing. But—knew what?"

"Rayburn—him and Carla Wayne. They're going to be married."

Even now, in a hotel room a thousand and more miles away, Ken could feel the blow after all these years. He sat in the bed, eyes fixed on darkness ahead, seeing the past and feeling every horrible moment of it.

He saw himself drop the glass. Like Rayburn, he had wheeled about and raced through the batwings. Wildly, he had plunged into the store, saw Carla was not there and had raced out again. A few moments later, he pounded on the door of her house, his fist shaking the whole structure.

It reluctantly opened and Carla's great dark eyes snapped fire at him. "Ken Ballard, what's the meaning of this!"

"You—you and Rayburn!" he blurted.

"What about it?"

He stared, brought up short and fearful by her cold words. "I heard—you and him—they said you were going to marry him."

"I am." Her voice softened just a trifle. "I would have told you, if you'd come in."

"But us! What about us?"

Her eyes hardened. "Chad—Mr. Rayburn—is a very handsome and acceptable man with an established future, and—"

"But I've got a spread. We planned to build it up and then—"

"Ken Ballard, do you call that bailing-wire outfit a ranch? The Double R Bar would make a hundred of it."

He felt frozen and said dully, "But you promised we'd be engaged and married."

"I promised nothing! Do you think I'd tie myself to a puncher with a few acres of land who thinks that makes him a rancher? I said I'd think it over. I have. What you've heard about Chad—Mr. Rayburn—and me should be answer enough. Good night, Mr. Ballard."

She closed the door in his face. A moment later it opened again and she smiled out at him. "Oh, and do come to the wedding. I want all my friends to be there."

He choked and took a half step toward her, but the door slammed again.

That had started the nightmare. From that moment life had been a meaningless blur, with only the moments of stress and pain all too clear. He recalled how he had stumbled blindly away and had gone to the store to talk to Mr. Wayne. He still could not quite believe what Carla had done.

Carla's father was even more insincerely polite

than his daughter had been. The marriage was a good one and Wayne obviously was already counting the profits from his daughter's union. Ken had left the store and ridden wildly home, like a crazy man, nearly killing the horse.

He tried to hold on to what was left, working the ranch, trying to bury himself in it. But nothing had meaning, and a day was no more than a succession of leaden, torturing hours. He finally returned to town. Carla and Rayburn, he heard, would be married the next Sunday. Ken heard it in the saloon and, sometime in the night, he found himself drunkenly singing and shouting to the stars.

Whiskey fumes stifled pain, dulled perception, freed him from Carla. Day followed day, all in a haze. He spent hard-earned money on liquor and lost some in card games that were only a blur. Then his pockets were empty and he could buy no more whiskey. He awoke stone cold sober Saturday morning in a livery-stable stall—sober and hate-filled. Rayburn had stolen his girl, and the man would be bound to come in today.

Ken waited, a gnawing pain and hatred nurturing patience. Midafternoon, the Double R Bar crew rode in, Rayburn leading them. Ken still waited until he could meet the man alone. That happened after Rayburn had spent an hour at Carla's home. He came whistling into the stable, leading his saddled horse. The whistle cut short when Ken stepped out from one of the stalls.

In a wild, slugging ten minutes, it was over. Chad Rayburn lay crumpled just within a stall, his lips smashed and his face bloody, his fine clothes mired by filth. Ken, breathing raggedly, had a cut lip and a swelling eye. He blew on his knuckles and looked down at the sprawled figure.

He no longer felt anger, only regret. Chad Rayburn had paid Carla Wayne's debt. Mind cleared and passions blasted away in the fight, Ken could see the situation clearly now. He could also see clearly that the Double R Bar outfit, headed by the arrogant elder Rayburn, would never let this pass. Ken would be lucky if he lived.

He swiped his hand across his bleeding lip. Money gone, girl gone, hopes and ambitions blasted, what was left? The ranch? He had no heart for it, even if the Rayburns allowed him to live. What was in the town? He shook his head and looked at Chad's still-saddled horse. He led it out, glanced along the momentarily deserted street, and then swung into saddle.

He did not bother to go to the ranch. Instead, he raced twenty miles to the small railroad town. He tied the horse at a rack before the main saloon and went to the railroad station, momentarily expecting to see vengeful Double R Bar riders. But an east-bound freight chugged in first. It dropped a cattle car and pulled out, with an unlisted passenger aboard. . . .

● ● ●

In the dark, boxlike room, Ken sighed and swung his legs out of the bed. He walked to the window, lifted the blind, and looked down on the sleeping street. From New Mexico to here—three years taken from his life and thrown away. Three years destroyed by Carla Wayne. He checked himself. No, he had also done what he could to destroy the little Carla had left. Thank God for that thin remaining core of self-respect. Like a slender steel rod, it had bent time and again but had never broken.

It was still bent, come to think about it. Not until he had found a way to pull out of this job without getting a bullet from a Moran gunslinger would he really be able to walk free and clear. Maybe then, somewhere, sometime, he could build his life again.

His eyes caught the dark saloon and he visualized Sparks' suspicious face. Ken smiled crookedly. Leave Alice Hanes alone—don't even look at her? After Carla Wayne, could he care for or trust any woman?

He turned back to the bed and dropped on it again. How little Sparks needed to worry! Ken stretched out. As though facing his memories had brought relief, sleep came almost instantly. But as his consciousness faded away, he dreamily looked into smoke-violet eyes.

VIII

Midafternoon of the first day of the return journey to Sioux Springs, Ken saw the rider approach as he rested the teams. There was something familiar about the figure, at a distance, and then Ken recognized Frank Sparks. Ken had taken the opportunity to stretch his cramped leg muscles, and now he leaned against a big wagon wheel waiting for the superintendent to come up.

In a few moments, Sparks drew rein. He flicked an eye at the horses and the long winding grade ahead where the road began to lift to the top of an abrupt rimrock. Sparks eased into the saddle, approving.

"You take care of your team, Ballard. I like that."

"They should have a chance to blow and rest before that long pull."

Sparks nodded, then lifted the reins. "Keep 'em rolling. With no deliveries or pick-ups, you should cut a day off the schedule."

"I'll be there."

"See that you are. After our talk, I figure you just might work out."

"Well, thanks."

"Forget it. But expect no favors. I don't work that way with any man."

Sparks made a curt gesture and, with a touch of spurs, set his horse in motion. He rode ahead up the grade that Ken would soon tackle. Ken watched him ride off, back straight and uncompromising. Finally Ken grunted and straightened, climbed back on the wagon seat.

The horses responded to his voice and the slap of the reins, and the heavy wagon started rolling. The animals set themselves to the long pull. Far ahead, Sparks was hardly more than a moving dot. Ken cuffed his hat back on his head. He knew what the brief exchange with Sparks had meant.

Sparks was jealous because of Alice Hanes, Ken thought, and rightly so. He was a tall, proud man—and touchy. Ken had aroused both his jealousy and his pride. The exchange in the saloon had partially allayed Sparks' antagonism—but only partially. He'd wait and see. His tone, attitude, and words showed that. Ken dismissed the man from his thoughts and pulled his eyes from the small, moving speck that topped the rim and then disappeared. . . .

The miles and the days rolled by slowly and uneventfully. Dawn of the third day found Ken not far from his destination. He should get into Sioux Springs around noon. He rolled his blankets, cooked breakfast and then lingered over the final tin cup of coffee. With a glance at the sun on the eastern horizon, he stood up and harnessed the horses, hitched them to the wagon.

He threw his bedroll under the seat, kicked dirt over his small fire. Then he turned—and stopped short. Tag Nixon sat his horse at the edge of the road.

Nixon grinned at Ken's surprised stare, and swung out of saddle. Ken realized the trees and the curve of the road had hidden the man until his approach to the turn-off where Ken had camped. Ken's attention to his own work had completed the surprise.

Nixon came up, looked down at the nearly obliterated fire. "I reckon you can take time to be sociable. Got up so early to meet you this morning that I could use some coffee."

"Must be important," Ken said shortly.

"You're always important to us, Ballard. Leastways, right now. How about the java?"

Ken pulled the pot and makings from the wagon, while Nixon revived the fire. Waiting for the coffee to boil, the gunman walked to the end of the wagon and pulled himself up so that he could look over the tailgate into the bed. Then he dropped back to the ground.

"Not much of a load."

"Return trip. Heavy going out." Ken poured the coffee and extended the tin cup. Nixon sipped gratefully, watching Ken over the rim.

A move of Nixon's eyes indicated the direction from which Ken had come. "Hanes got a lot of business up that way?"

"I don't know. My first trip. Full load going up, not much coming back."

"Well, that's enough. Like your job?"

"Sure, but not the reason for taking it."

"Now what's wrong with it? You just tell me what goes on, and that's all."

"Is it? I figure you and Moran know enough as it is. You don't need me out on a wagon."

Nixon lowered the cup and his face grew tight. "Why not?"

"A man in Sioux Springs, watching that station, could tell how many wagons leave and how busy Hanes is. A ride north to where I been, and a couple days' watching, would tell you the business that station does. You've got something else planned for me."

"Such as?"

Ken angrily shrugged his shoulders. "I don't know. It won't be good."

"You can quit," Nixon said softly.

Ken's dry laugh snapped the short silence. "Quit, sure—and die."

"That's right. We've all gone too far to upset anything now." Nixon hunkered before the fire and refilled his cup. He straightened and his heavy face lost its harsh lines. "You worry too much, Ballard. Information—that's all we want."

"Such as?"

"Well, take that man Sparks. Is he as tough and hard as we've heard?"

"A driver," Ken admitted. "Touchy."

"You and him had words?"

"Well—" Ken hesitated and then saw no reason to hold back—"in a way. He don't like me."

"Why?"

"Personal, mostly. He figured I looked too much at Alice Hanes."

"Did he now!" Nixon's brow arched and then his eyes suddenly narrowed. "Did you?"

"No more'n anyone. I told him I wanted no woman to tangle things up."

"And now?"

"He ain't sure he'll believe me yet. But he will."

Nixon took another deep gulp of the coffee and then threw the remainder aside. He gave the cup to Ken. "Alice Hanes, eh? Sparks is jealous of her?"

"Some."

Nixon said suggestively, "Most men wouldn't mind sparking a girl as pretty as that'n. Would you?"

Ken kicked dirt over the fire again, thoroughly smothering it this time. He finally looked up. "Anything else you got in mind?"

For a moment Nixon seemed as if he'd argue, and then a secretive, thoughtful look came into his eyes. "No, nothing. Just keep driving. I reckon Brad will have an idea or two."

"Not about Alice Hanes—or any woman."

"Friend, you sure hate skirts!"

"Let's say I did once. Right now, I don't care one way or another."

Nixon hitched at his gunbelt and turned to his horse. He swung into saddle, lifted the reins, looked down at Ken. "I'll be gone for a while. When I get in touch again, I'll want to know how Hanes is doing."

"Like I said, just keep a man watching in town. You don't need me."

"Let Brad decide about that."

Nixon wheeled his horse around and rode off in the direction of Sioux Springs.

As Ken had expected, he sighted the distant buildings of the town around noon. The horses, sensing the end of the long journey, picked up speed and the big freighting wagon lumbered smartly into town, down the main street and into the busy station yard.

By the time Ken had unhitched the horses and turned them over to the hostler, and had given his manifests to the foreman, another hour had passed. Lou Hanes and Alice drove into the yard in a buggy. The girl descended at the office door but her eyes lighted on Ken, who stood on the distant dock.

Lou drove on to the stable, turned horse and buggy over to a hostler and then came to the dock. He nodded at Ken. "How was the trip?"

"All right. No trouble, but I reckon Sparks told you. Saw him up there, and again on the road."

"Frank said you might work out," Hanes admitted. "I know I'm satisfied to keep you on the payroll."

"Until Jake Lacey's back?"

"Regular, even after Jake returns. He's coming along, by the way. The way hauling's picking up, I've been thinking of putting another wagon on the run over Treachery Pass to Pass City."

"I'd think an older hand would get a main run like that," Ken said, surprised.

"Well, yes. But now we're shorthanded. Anyway, we figure to try you out on the run."

"We?" Ken picked up the word. "You and Sparks?"

"Frank's down Pass City way himself. No, Alice and me. She's a pretty good judge, I've found."

Words of refusal formed on Ken's lips but he choked them back. He had an idea what Sparks would do when he heard of the change. The Haneses, father and daughter, would not risk losing their superintendent because of a quarrel over a teamster. Ken suddenly saw this as a means to a quick end to this job. Moran or Nixon couldn't blame him if Sparks had him fired.

Hanes obviously expected response. Ken smiled quietly. "Thanks for the chance."

Hanes frowned, swiftly erased it. "Day after tomorrow you'll start the trip. Full load going and coming. Check in at the office before you leave today."

When Hanes left, the foreman said softly, "You're drawing an important run right off."

"Think I'll keep it?" Ken snapped.

"There's a good chance. Lou backs Miss Alice and, after all, they own the freight line. Frank's just a hired hand like the rest of us. But . . ." His voice drifted off.

Ken read the troubled expression and nodded. "Yeah, rub Sparks the wrong way and what happens?"

"It won't be good," the man admitted.

Ken jumped down off the dock and crossed to the office. He spent nearly half an hour there. He was paid for his first week and again had to work up a passable appearance of pleasure at the new run he was to make. He noticed Alice's puzzled, half-angry frown, but chose to disregard it. He pocketed his pay and turned to the door.

The girl checked him. "Do you plan to stay on at the hotel, Mr. Ballard?"

"Hadn't given it much thought, but I'll look around some."

"Tomorrow will be a good time—your day off."

"Yes, ma'am."

He bobbed his head and hastily retreated. He walked out of the station yard, frowning, and the frown was still with him when he turned in at the hotel. It would seem that Alice Hanes took an interest in him, and that could easily lead to trouble with Sparks. But more to the point, her attraction bothered Ken. He wanted no such entanglement as this. Then his face cleared. Why should he worry? Once Sparks caught on, he'd be free of the job and free of the girl's unwanted attention. Let the string play out.

Despite Alice's suggestion, Ken loafed in his hotel room most of the next day. He had a few drinks that night, turned in early and was up at dawn. As he had expected, she was not at the station at such an early hour. Relieved, he climbed onto the heavily loaded wagon and tooled it out to the street and south toward the distant Treachery Range.

The town and the girl behind him, he felt momentarily free and set himself for the long trip. He grinned when he suddenly wondered what Nixon and Moran would think, seeing him in Pass City. His grin grew wider as he pictured their expressions when he would, inevitably and through no fault of his own, be fired.

He'd shake the dust of this whole country from his boots. But he'd not go back to the railroads and hobo jungles again. He had a start on a new trail and, somewhere, he intended to keep on riding it. Alone, of course.

The heavy wagon moved slowly and, once again, Ken made camp, now in the broken foothills of the mountain range. The next day the road began to lift and twist toward the high pass. Speed decreased and there were times when

Ken crawled upward, envious of the stagecoach that came whirling by on the descent to the valley he had left behind.

Camp again, this time among pines, and man and horses took a much needed rest. The next morning he was still climbing, until at last the road leveled out into the pass itself. The animals tossed their heads, snorted as though in triumph, and the wagon rolled faster.

Traffic along this main road northward was surprisingly light for the moment. An hour or more passed as Ken tooled the wagon around the sweeping curves. Sun glinted on the high peaks above and made golden, slanting streamers between the tall trees that grew thick on either side.

He rounded a turn and saw a rider ahead, coming toward him. He and Sparks recognized one another at the same instant. Sparks' jaw dropped and he reined in abruptly at the side of the road. Ken did not check his teams but rolled on, lifting his whip in greeting as the wagon lumbered by the frozen man on the horse.

A few seconds later, Ken heard the rapid beat of hoofs. Sparks raced up from behind, glared at him. "Pull over."

Ken reined the teams to the side of the road and stopped on a grassy shoulder. Sparks came up again, glaring. "What are you doing on this run?"

"They gave it to me."

"A new man like you! I'll have the hide of the man who did this!"

Ken choked back his inclination to grin. This was working exactly as he had hoped. Sparks cursed, then said, "I ought to turn you around and send you back! I'm the one who assigns drivers and—"

"Maybe Lou didn't know that," Ken cut in mildly.

Sparks' mouth snapped shut and his dark eyes glittered as he studied Ken angrily. Then they revealed a new and mounting suspicion. His voice flattened, tightened. "Did you persuade Lou?"

"Now wait. When I come in from that last run, Lou put me on this one."

"Why?"

Ken shook his head. "Maybe you can ask the boss why, but I can't. He said he and Miss Alice—"

"Her!" Sparks' face flamed and he leaned out of the saddle toward Ken, glaring up at him. "So you worked your way around her!"

Ken shook his head. "You're reading sign backward. Lou told me when I came in from the north trip. Don't blame me for it."

Sparks slowly straightened. His dark face was still tight, though now he had gained control of his explosive anger. But the jealous suspicion still flamed in every line of jaw, mouth and eyes. "All right, Ballard, I'll find out just how it happened. You can bet on that."

He lifted the reins and, with a cruel dig of the spurs, pulled his horse around and thundered off. Ken craned around the canvas cover of the wagon to looked after him. He had a vanishing glimpse of a black silhouette in a cloud of dust. The fading roll of hoofs came back to him. Ken straightened, faced forward toward Pass City. This job, he decided, would last just about till his return to Sioux Springs. He cheerfully urged the horses with a word and a snap of the whip.

He helped unload the wagon at the big busy station in Pass City. Here, as in some of the other towns, Hanes had arranged hotel accommodations for his drivers. Ken checked in, washed the dust of the journey away, and looked down on the busy street. He heard the whistle of a switch locomotive in the far-off railroad yards. His eyes grew distant, and he nodded.

Call to the far places, he thought, and soon he would answer it. He'd buy a ticket anywhere yonderly, away from Alice Hanes, Tag Nixon and Brad Moran. Maybe he'd hire on at a ranch, punching again. Maybe he'd freight—something. Either way, he'd be free again and could shape his life as he liked.

Thought of Nixon and Moran made him drum his fingers absentmindedly on the window sill. If he were fired by Sparks, there could be a chance one of Moran's gundogs might pull a trigger without waiting to ask questions. It'd be like

Nixon, for instance, to do that. Maybe he'd better let Moran know how things were shaping up. He turned from the window, snatched his hat from the bed, and walked out.

Not long afterward, he stood in Moran's private office. Brad leaned back in his chair before his desk and narrowly eyed Ken, while Tag Nixon straddled a chair across the room. They had recovered from the surprise they had showed when Ken first walked into the main office. Now Moran considered the news about Sparks.

His eyes had that strange flick and were still as cold gray as Ken remembered. Finally, he slapped his hand on the desk with an air of finality and surrender. "All right, Ballard; if you lose the job, you lose it. We didn't figure on the setup. But hold onto the job as long as you can."

"Why not quit here in Pass City and beat Sparks to the punch?" Ken asked mildly.

"Because we don't know yet that he can get you fired," Moran snapped. "You're guessing, though I admit you might not be wrong. If Sparks doesn't swing enough weight with the Haneses, then keep on freighting. Either way, Tag or I will be up at Sioux Springs and you'll get orders."

Ken hid his disappointment, thinking that he had plans of his own. He shrugged in agreement and walked out.

When he had left, Moran slowly turned his head and looked at Nixon. The gunslinger waited, eyes questioning. Moran suddenly smiled, a cruel move of the lips. "Well, what do you know! Real luck!"

"How do we work it?" Nixon asked.

"Sparks will work it for us. We don't have to bother." Moran chuckled again and stood up, shoving his hands deep in his pockets as he paced thoughtfully from desk to the window and back again.

After a moment he said, "Ride out tonight, Tag. Keep a close watch in Sioux Springs. When you see the thing's worked to a blow-up, or Ballard's fired, you know what to do."

Nixon nodded, eyes glowing. Moran dropped into his chair again. "No slip-up, Tag—and make sure our friend gets all the credit. Sparks and that girl will be ready to believe any signs. You know where they should point."

Nixon stood up and hitched at his gunbelt. "I know, and you can depend on it."

He went to the door and had just touched the knob when Moran's voice checked him. When he turned, Moran's eyes glowed exultantly. "Moran wagons north of the Treachery Range—and no others! Tag, I could be in a mighty generous mood after this is over."

Nixon chuckled, but his voice held an edge of sharpness. "I'll remind you."

IX

A few days later, Ken drove into the station yard at Sioux Springs. The wagon was loaded to capacity, and strung out along the miles behind him were three more, bearing goods from the rail lines to the towns and ranches fanning north and west from the Treachery Range. It was an indication of the lucrative business Hanes controlled, and Ken could now readily understand Moran's desire to own or to cut in.

He expertly swung, cut, and backed the big wagon to the dock, jumped down from the seat and stretched cramped muscles. The foreman looked up from his check stand and Ken grinned, waved a greeting. The man answered, but there was something worried and withdrawn in his eyes.

He accepted the sheaf of manifests Ken handed him, hesitated, then glanced toward the office. "What've you said or done to Frank?"

"Nothing."

"He's sure worked up a mad about you. I told you to walk wide and talk soft. They want you in the office as soon as you come in, they said."

Ken turned away and jumped off the dock. As he walked across the yard, he felt certain he would be paid off and dismissed. Probably Sparks would be there, on the prod. But Ken felt he could hold his tongue and temper this short remaining time. It would be a small price to pay for release.

He opened the door and stepped into the office. Sparks was not present. Both Lou Hanes and Alice looked up from their desks and Ken instantly saw the troubled shadows that momentarily appeared in their eyes.

Alice shot a look at her father, who stood up and came to the barrier. "How did it go, Ballard?"

"No trouble that I know of."

"Fine! Fine! Alice, you have his wages ready?"

She opened a drawer and took out a small envelope, passed it to her father, who gave it to Ken. He moistened his lips, and Ken was sure the man was bracing himself to say the job was over.

But his words surprised Ken. "Day after tomorrow you'll take out another load. We're sending you west this time." He saw Ken's surprise and misunderstood it. He said hastily, "We've decided—all of us—to have you drive all our routes before we decide where we'll use you."

Ken looked at the silent girl, back at Hanes. "What does Sparks think of this?"

Lou flushed, but the girl's body jerked proudly and angrily erect. "Frank abides by our decisions!"

"Yes, ma'am."

She flushed, reading his meaning. "It's true he didn't think you were ready for the important Pass City route yet and . . . we followed his advice there."

"So we'll rotate you," Hanes cut in hastily.

Ken hesitated, shrugged. "So long as it's all right with Sparks."

"It will be; it is," Alice said flatly.

He gave father and daughter a long, searching, and sceptical look, then touched his hatbrim and left. He walked through the gate and onto the street before he thoughtfully looked back at the station.

He could guess what had happened. Sparks must have kicked up a big storm when he came in from Pass City. He'd been mad that they'd gone over his head, and that blind jealousy of his would have been riding him. Sparks had undoubtedly demanded that Ken be fired, and then the fire-works had started.

Ken could picture it. Hanes was a just man and his daughter a proud woman. For different motives, neither would accede to Sparks' demands. So there had been a final compromise, Ken's new route.

Reaching his hotel, Ken went up to his room and looked down on the street, baffled. He was still on a job he didn't want. He thought of Moran, Nixon, and their gunhawks, and knew he did not dare to walk off the job yet. They'd figure he'd lied to Moran about being fired, and that could be dangerous for Ken. But he wanted to get out of this—safely.

If only Sparks had had his way! Suddenly Ken's eyes lighted. Maybe, with a little persuasion,

Sparks could have his way. Ken considered the idea, turned it over and then, with a deep chuckle, turned back into the room and peeled off his shirt.

About midmorning the next day, Ken lazily walked into the station yard. The early loads had gone out and the men in the warehouse now moved about at odd jobs. The foreman looked surprised when Ken mounted the steps to the dock. Just beyond him, Sparks turned and saw Ken.

His handsome face tightened and the set of his lips showed distaste. "What are you doing here, Ballard?"

"Time on my hands, so I thought I'd check the new route now instead of in the morning. Then I want to see Miss Alice."

Sparks' brows drew down. "What for?"

"Something personal," Ken answered lightly.

He turned to the foreman, aware that Sparks stared, fists clenched at his side. Disregarding the man, Ken asked questions of the foreman about the western route. He felt the boring eyes of the superintendent like a weight between his shoulder blades.

After getting his answers, Ken thanked the foreman and, without so much as a glance at Sparks, jumped down off the dock.

"Ballard!"

Ken turned, looked back up at Sparks. The man

stood tense, legs slightly spread, eyes glittering down at Ken, who asked mildly, "Yes?"

Sparks' mouth opened, and then he realized the foreman was watching and listening just behind him. Sparks snapped his lips shut, a muscle jumping in his cheek. "Nothing. Talk about it tomorrow."

Ken waited a second and then turned away. He walked to the office, feeling the angry glare of jealous eyes again. He entered the office to find Alice alone at her desk. Ken closed the door with care behind him, seeing Sparks still poised on the edge of the dock.

He turned to the girl then, abruptly, and surprised a strange, soft look in her eyes. An instant later it was gone; she spoke crisply. "Mr. Ballard, I hardly expected to see you today."

He took off his hat. "I've been thinking about moving out of the hotel, ma'am, like you said. I thought maybe you might know of a place."

Her face lighted with pleasure. "I think you're wise." She arose and came to the railing, so close that he caught the clean pleasant perfume she wore. "Do you want a small house, or a room with someone?"

"Well, a house means furniture." His ears strained toward the door. "Maybe a room would be best. Do you know of any?"

She nodded. Just then the door opened behind Ken and he heard a heavy step. Alice looked beyond him and then deliberately at Ken. "Try

Mrs. O'Brian—that big white house down the street. Or there's Mrs. Jason, over two streets. I hear she's been taking roomers."

Sparks pushed open the barrier gate and walked heavily to Hanes' desk. He looked through a stack of shipping memos, his face tight.

Ken smiled at the girl. "Thank you, ma'am. I sure appreciate this. Maybe I can return the favor some time."

"There's no need." She gave him a warm smile and, for a brief second, Ken was lost in the depths of smoke-violet eyes. He caught himself.

"Anyhow, thanks," he said in a muffled voice, and hurried to the door and out.

He walked quickly away from the station, still seeing those beautiful eyes and the full lips shaped to the warm smile. He could still feel the impact shaking him. Abruptly he cut across the street and plunged into a saloon.

The fiery taste of the whiskey broke the spell. But he stared wonderingly at his reflection in the backbar mirror. What drew him so strongly to Alice Hanes? It didn't make sense, and he didn't like it. Here he planned a lone-wolf life, told himself he'd never trust another woman, but a smile, a voice, violet eyes, threatened everything.

He tossed off the remainder of the drink and pushed away from the bar. Returning to the street, he hesitated, looking back toward the station. Maybe he should find a room, work for the Haneses, be near the girl. It would be easy to do.

He grunted. Fool! He was Moran's spy and sooner or later, in one way or another, that would come out. A slip of the tongue, a glimpse of Nixon with him, maybe some move by Moran himself. Then what would happen to all these fine, loco ideas? He turned away, grinning crookedly. He was about to fall into the trap he himself had set for Sparks.

He visited Mrs. O'Brian and Mrs. Jason, glanced briefly at the neat, clean rooms and said he might return. He spent the rest of the afternoon in the hotel, had supper and then went to the saloon next door. He nodded to the few men he knew, station workers, and ordered a drink at the bar. He had now put Alice Hanes where she belonged in his mind—a lovely woman who would soon be a part of his past, no more than a chance acquaintance.

He ordered his second drink and, chancing to glance in the mirror, saw Hank Scatlin. The gunman's pinched face remained bland as he met Ken's eyes. They might have been complete strangers. But Ken felt a slight chill. Moran was on the alert, and Ken had been right not to quit his job. Word spread in a small town like this and the man over there could be executioner as easily as not.

Ken felt someone brush in beside him and

looked around into Sparks' dark face. The glittering eyes held his a moment; then Sparks calmly ordered a drink. Despite outward appearances, Ken sensed the man's inner tension.

Sparks tossed down the drink, ordered another. Then he turned his head to look at Ken. "Did you find a room today?"

"Haven't decided."

Sparks held his voice level and low. "I didn't think you would. It was for her benefit, wasn't it?"

"Well, now as to that——"

"Don't lie, Ballard. I don't know how, but you got around her enough to get the Pass City run. Now you ask her about a place to live, like you're helpless or Sioux Springs is as big as Frisco and you're lost."

Ken said nothing. In the mirror he saw Scatlin sharply eye them, sensing, with his gunman's instinct, that something was wrong. The sight of the man steeled Ken to grab this unexpected opportunity Sparks had unwittingly given him. From the corner of his eye, Ken saw the tendons stand out tightly in Sparks' clenched hand.

"What makes you think I'm lying?" Ken asked. "I figure on staying here and driving for the Haneses."

Sparks jerked visibly, fought for and found control. His voice came tight and low. "You might live here, but you won't drive for Hanes. I'll see to it."

Ken gave him a level look. "Maybe Lou will have something to say about that . . . or Miss Alice."

Sparks nearly choked. "Ballard, why don't you make it easy on yourself and just ride out—tonight?"

"I never walk off a job."

"Then you might be carried off this one. You've had your warning. You'd be wise if you didn't show up tomorrow morning."

Ken shrugged, a gesture he knew infuriated Sparks. "I'll see how I feel, come morning."

Sparks savagely pushed away from the bar. He glared at Ken, became aware that the men along the bar stared curiously at him. Then he took a deep breath. "If that's how you want it."

He turned on his heel, heedlessly brushed a man aside and strode out of the saloon. Ken lifted his finger to signal for another drink and set himself to the bar. His face remained calm but within he felt tight. He knew he had pushed Sparks to the edge of violence. Tomorrow he'd have to go further. A hell of a way to lose a job, he thought.

He finished the drink. Scatlin had disappeared a few moments before. Ken could picture the man going to Nixon with the story of the brush with Sparks. But that was also part of the plan.

When Ken stepped out on the saloon porch, he saw the gunman standing near the steps. The man turned as Ken came up. "Got a match, friend?"

Ken stopped, fished in his pocket. Scatlin spoke in a low voice. "Frank Sparks sure ain't no friend of yours."

"Did Nixon tell you?"

"Yeah, but I could see for myself," Scatlin said smugly, and accepted the match.

"He hates my guts," Ken answered with a pretended growl. "He says he's going to get me fired. Tell Nixon I'll hang on as long as I can, but I'll be lucky to be on the payroll tomorrow."

"I'll tell him." Scatlin's voice lifted as men came out of the saloon. "Thanks for the match, friend."

Ken waved it aside, descended the steps to the street, walked toward the hotel. So Nixon was somewhere around the town! His gundog had seen the incident at the bar. Now they expected trouble. In the morning, Ken thought grimly, I'll see that Sparks makes it.

The sun stood just above the horizon the next morning when Ken walked into the station yard. All the wagons but his had pulled out and he saw Sparks angrily talking to Lou Hanes at the dock. The two men turned when Ken, after a deep breath, moved unconcernedly toward the stable.

"Ballard!"

Ken checked, turned to face the superintendent. Sparks stepped forward. "You should've been here an hour ago."

"What's an hour on a four-five day run? It can be made up."

He turned away but Sparks grabbed his arm, swung him back around. "You act like you don't care about this job, Ballard. We can sure find someone else."

Hanes cut in. "Frank, let it go. As he said, what's an hour?"

Sparks glared at Ken for a long moment, then reluctantly released him. Ken defiantly shrugged his sleeve back into place and turned again to the stable. He harnessed and brought out the teams. Hanes now stood in the office doorway, Sparks at the wagon Ken was to drive.

As Ken came up with the horses, Sparks snapped, "This cargo will shift, Ballard. It'll have to be reloaded."

Ken moved the horses to the wagon without comment. He hitched them as Sparks watched, fuming. Then he straightened and stepped to the wagon, preparing to climb to the seat. Sparks lunged forward, swung him about.

"I said the cargo will shift."

Ken eyed him levelly, inwardly pleased that the plan was working, outwardly giving a show of quiet defiance. His voice was low, carrying only to Sparks. "Do you have to hunt around for a reason to get rid of me? Haven't you got the nerve to come right out and fire me? Or maybe you're the one who wants to prove to Miss Alice—"

Sparks' lips drew back over his teeth as his eyes blazed. He breathed heavily, glaring. Ken made a contemptuous gesture. "I figured you were more of a man than this, finding some little fault—"

The cut of the words, the curl that Ken's lips deliberately formed, snapped the last faint check Sparks held on his temper. He swung without warning. Ken jerked his head aside, but the heavy fist grazed along his chin, sending him off balance and back.

He struck the ground, heard Lou's shout of alarm. Ken came catlike to his feet and Sparks charged in, blind mad with fury. His tempestuous rush drove Ken back. A second blow thudded off Ken's ribs and he gasped at the shocking pain of it. He countered a third blow, gave ground. He had not counted on an actual fight—did not want one. He hoped Lou or some of the men on the dock would break it up.

Sparks swung and his first smashed along the side of Ken's head. Lights flashed and suddenly Ken no longer cared about sparing Sparks. If the man wanted a fight, he'd get one. Ken caught his balance and his blow slugged deep into Sparks' stomach.

The man doubled up, but had enough wits left to move aside as Ken tried to end the fight with a smashing blow to the chin. Sparks fell into a clinch, carrying Ken back. Ken tried to break loose, but Sparks held on grimly. Suddenly Ken's back struck the high dock. Sparks, breath regained, straightened. His blow whipped by Ken's jaw, missing it by a whisper.

Ken dimly heard shouts close by. He was grabbed by a dozen hands and he saw men swarm over Sparks, pulling him back. Ken instantly dropped his arms. Sparks tried to shake off the restraining hands that held him. Lou Hanes stepped between the two groups.

"Frank! Get hold of yourself!"

Sparks glared, then slowly straightened. He shook off the restraining hands and, breathing raggedly, gasped, "All right, the fight's over."

The other men released Ken, who rubbed his hand along his jaw. Hanes looked from one to the other in helpless anger. "Now what was that all about?"

"What's it matter?" Sparks growled. "I'm firing this man."

"Why?" Hanes demanded.

"I gave him an order about his load. He wouldn't obey it. That's enough for me, Lou. He's fired, or I quit."

Hanes glanced at Ken, back at Sparks. Before Hanes could speak, Ken cut in. "I reckon that tells me where I stand. There's always other jobs."

Hanes looked at him again and lifted his shoulders, let them fall. Ken pushed through the group and Sparks turned to watch him. Ken walked to the wagon, scooped his fallen hat from the ground, turned to the gate.

Alice Hanes stood just within the yard. Ken's stride broke a second and then he set his jaw and came on. The violet eyes looked questioningly at him. It took an effort for Ken to look away and walk out of the yard.

Ken went immediately to his hotel room. He stripped off jacket and ripped shirt and gingerly washed the bruises on his face and jaw. He straightened, looking at himself in the mirror, seeing the marks Sparks' fists had made. He grimaced, knowing he had made a poor showing except for those last few seconds when sudden anger at the blows had made him strike back instead of merely defending himself.

He turned abruptly away. If Hanes and the others had jumped in faster, the fight would have been stopped almost before it started. Yet he blamed himself for the fight. He had spurred Sparks just enough to make the man explode in violence. Why? Ken wondered. Because Alice Hanes was in the back of his mind? Because he was unknowingly jealous of Sparks?

Ken tried to reject the thought but did not wholly succeed. The girl's faint image remained in his thoughts like a ghost as he looked about the bare room and considered his next move. He wanted to leave the town immediately, but felt it would be best to wait until morning. By then the gossip of the station workers around town and in the saloon would spread the story of the fight and his firing.

To gather up his things now and ride out before Scatlin and Nixon heard the news might be a wrong and fatal move. Now, fired at last, he could afford to wait. So, fully clothed, Ken stretched out on the bed, stared up at the ceiling and considered where he would start his life anew.

Less than an hour later he was startled by a knock on the door. He swung his legs to the floor and, crossing the room, wondered if word had already reached Nixon. He opened the door and his eyes rounded.

Alice Hanes stood in the dark hallway. She met his amazed stare and her chin lifted a little as she asked calmly, "May I come in?"

He caught himself, stepped hastily back and waved her in. She swept regally into the room, a single sweep of her eyes registering everything in it. Ken hastily closed the door and pulled the chair out from the wall.

Her tight smile thanked him as she sat down. Ken uncertainly moved to the bed and sank down on its edge. She spoke crisply. "I've surprised you, Mr. Ballard."

"Yes, ma'am!" He frowned, glancing toward the door. "Did anyone see you?"

"You're thinking of gossip," she cut in. "I'm also aware of that chance, and I'm willing to risk it."

"Why?"

"I want to know the truth about your fight with Frank."

"Why, as to that," he said slowly, "I reckon Sparks told you."

"He said you refused to obey an order, that you insulted him and he lost his temper. I can believe Frank lost his temper, but I'm not sure of the rest. No one but you and Frank knows what went on between you just before the fight. I've heard his story. I want to hear yours."

Ken hesitated, uncertain what to tell her. He hardly dared look at her; her presence disturbed him badly. He heard the rustle of her skirt, her small sigh.

"Perhaps I should explain a few things," she said. "I'll be honest. Frank apparently took a dislike to you the night the posse tried to catch those outlaws. Frank's hot tempered, impetuous. He would've ridden off in all directions that night to no purpose. My father and the sheriff told me about it. Unluckily for you, the sheriff used you to back his arguments."

"He didn't need to. The sign was there."

"But Frank didn't want to see it." She made a small, impatient gesture. "Oh, he saw it well enough, but by then he had already talked too wide about getting the outlaws there and then. He simply couldn't allow himself to be mistaken. The sheriff proved him wrong, and made you support it. No drifting stranger could do that to Frank."

"I guess we're all a little like that, ma'am."

"Perhaps, but only a little." She lost some of her confidence, considered her folded hands for a moment and then regained determination. "I may as well tell the whole truth, Mr. Ballard. I am sure Frank thinks that he and I will be married sometime. There has been nothing said, and perhaps it's my fault he feels that way. I admit I have thought of it, but—" she broke off momentarily—"not seriously. Frank has."

"Maybe he should know how you feel," Ken said shortly.

She flushed. "I admit it. But I just haven't wanted to bring it to a head. It would be unpleasant and . . . we can't afford to lose such a good superintendent. Father wouldn't know what to do without him."

Ken said, out of bitter memories, "One way or another, a man gets over something like that."

She looked curiously at him, seemed about to question him, and then changed her mind. "I'm saying, Mr. Ballard, that Frank's jealous of you. I helped that along because I thought you'd make a top driver, and put you on the Pass City run without talking to Frank. You didn't know it, but when you asked me about the rooms for rent, you built up his jealousy."

Ken almost said he *had* known it, but bit back the words. Alice said tightly, "Now that you understand these things, Mr. Ballard, will you tell me why you and Frank had the fight?"

For a wild moment, Ken wanted to tell her the truth. Those crazy thoughts and dreams came rushing back. But only for a moment. He was less than a year from a useless life and the hobo jungles. He had nothing but a driver's wages to offer, and she paid those wages. He saw Carla Wayne. He saw Brad Moran, and Tag Nixon's way of rubbing his fingers along his holster. The impulse to tell the truth died when weighed against these realities.

The words came with difficulty, as though he had been forced to acknowledge wrong. "He gave me an order. I told him I wouldn't do it. You heard the story right from him—all of it."

"I see."

After a moment she said, "That's all?"

"That's all."

Absently she smoothed her skirt. "I guess I have my answer, don't I? I'm disappointed in you. There was something about you that seemed dependable, and I'm not often wrong."

"I'm a drifter, ma'am. You never saw me before and you knew nothing about me. I reckon you won't see me again."

She forced a faint smile and stood up. He jumped to his feet and went ahead to open the door. She hesitated. "I'm sorry, Mr. Ballard."

"So am I."

She bit her lip and then swept through the

doorway and disappeared. He remained in the opening, hearing the fading tap of her steps down the hall. Then there was only silence. He slowly closed the door, turned and stood quite still for a long moment. Then he slammed his fist into his palm and dropped down on the bed.

The remaining hours of the day dragged dully. That evening, Ken ate a lonely supper and returned to his room. He lit the lamp, pulled down the shade and looked distastefully about the cubicle. Come tomorrow morning, he'd leave this place and this town for good.

He heard faint steps in the hallway and his attention sharpened as they halted just outside his door. Then he heard a soft, secretive tapping. He crossed the room and threw open the door. Hank Scatlin stepped in.

Ken closed the door. "What do you want?"

The gunman dropped into the chair as though he had been made welcome. "I heard about what happened this morning. I reckon you called the cards."

Ken hid relief and a feeling of success. Nixon would know by now, and Ken could almost se the trail to freedom and a new life clear before him. His voice lost its sharpness. "Sparks fired me. Hanes let it stand."

"So I hear." Scatlin looked about the room, his eyes darting here and there. "Tag wants to see you."

"Any time."

"Now. I'll take you to him. He's waiting along the Pass City road."

Ken hid impatience. Why couldn't they accept the loss of the job and let him go? He pulled his gunbelt from the dresser drawer and buckled it on, shrugged into his coat and picked up his hat.

The two men left the room and the hotel. The gunman's horse stood at the hotel hitchrack and he swung under the rail, untied the reins. "Your horse at the stable? I'll meet you there."

Ken walked on. A few moments later he rode out of the town livery and Scatlin came up beside him on the dark street. Without a word they headed south toward Treachery Pass. Few lights showed in the scattered houses. Soon the town was behind them, the darkness of the open range was enfolding them.

A half mile or so out, a shadow moved and a horseman materialized from the black shadows of the trees. "Hank?"

"That's right, Tag. Ballard's with me."

Nixon came up and Ken saw the white blur of his face in the dim light. "Tell me about it, Ballard. Hank, get back to town. I'll see you later."

Scatlin reined about and faded into the darkness. Nixon again faced Ken and asked for the details. Ken told him what had happened, omitting his goading of Sparks. Nixon listened quietly until the end.

"Okay, Ballard, it couldn't be helped."

"Then you'll not want me around anymore?"

"No, you're finished. But Brad's satisfied. Head into Pass City tomorrow and he'll pay you what he owes you."

"Owes me?"

"Brad said at the beginning you'd be on his payroll all the time." Nixon lifted the reins. "He keeps his word, so you got wages coming if you want to collect 'em. After that you can go anywhere—including hell—as far as Brad's concerned. Any objections?"

"Of course not. I just never figured—"

"Like I said, Brad pays in full for what he buys. You head out tomorrow, you'll get your pay that much sooner. Being a drifter, I reckon you could use it. See you sometime."

He lifted his hand and drifted off into the shadows again. Ken heard the faint sound of hoofs and then silence. He reined about himself and headed back toward town.

Early the next morning, after breakfast, he packed his things. Socks, neckerchiefs, underwear, he picked up in small bundles out of the dresser drawers, wrapped them up in his saddle roll. He went to the small closet where his rifle stood. He picked it up without pulling it from leather, thinking what a waste of money the weapon had been so far. He half pulled the rifle from the scabbard and then let it drop back.

Maybe somewhere along this trip he'd fire it, if only at a coyote or a buzzard.

Shortly thereafter, he carried his bedroll and rifle to the livery stable, saddled his horse and rode out onto the street. Giving a long, searching look toward the distant station, he could picture Alice seated at her desk. He touched spurs, a bit hard, and the horse lunged forward with a snort. Ken pulled it in and rode out of Sioux Springs at an easy pace. He had plenty of time to reach his destination, wherever it might be.

He headed south toward the Treachery Range and the long, winding pass through it. For a time, the distant peaks on the far horizon seemed to be a goal and then, suddenly, he realized that for the first time in many years he was free. It was not the meaningless freedom of degradation he had known. That was merely drifting, like a dead leaf on a murky stream of water.

He slowed the pace of the horse and relaxed, swaying easily to the animal's movement. His freedom now was that of choice, of making his life what he willed. No Carla Waynes to tear it apart now, no Brad Morans to force him to a job, no Alice Haneses to distract with half-formed dreams that could never be anything but hopeless.

The remainder of the day he drifted along, and the twilight shadows found him just within the mouth of Treachery Pass. This close to the high and looming peaks, the night pressed down swiftly, although out on the plains there was still a false suggestion of day.

Ken found a pleasant swale leading back into the trees, thought he heard the distant burble of water. He reined off the road and followed the faint sound. It grew stronger as the trees thickened and the road behind him was lost to sight. He pushed through a thin screen of bushes and drew rein. Grass sloped down to the edge of a little mountain stream and Ken nodded with satisfaction when he looked around at a place that was a perfect camping ground for the night.

He picketed the horse, off-saddled, and spread his bedroll. He built a small fire, its flame growing brighter and stronger as the shadows deepened and full night came. Beans, bacon, and coffee, then a lazy time before the fire, now and then throwing a small branch on it. Alone under the stars, he basked in his freedom.

Once he straightened, his ears keened back to the road. He had heard a faint, rolling sound back there that swiftly faded somewhere to the south. Ken frowned, trying to place the noise. It sounded something like a party of riders going at break-neck speed. But the silence of the night remained unbroken and, at last, he rolled into his blankets.

Sleep came easily, induced by the low singing of the stream, the soft sounds of the horse at graze on the picket rope. He did not awaken until sun sent long golden shafts through the tops of the trees into his eyes.

He looked on a bright sunny world with the invigorating nip of early morning in the high country. Rolling out of his blankets, he washed his face and hands in the clear cold water of the stream. The fire had died and he built it up. When the flames died again, he placed coffee pot and frying pan over the embers. He whistled softly as he watched bacon sizzle and breathed in the aroma of the coffee.

He heard a slight, foreign sound behind him and he started to turn his head. A harsh voice, filled with hatred, broke the silence of the place.

"Don't move, you damn killer—or you'll get a bullet in the back, just like you gave Lou Hanes!"

XI

Ken couldn't help the spasmodic jerk of his nerves. He controlled his voice and the impulse to turn his head, kept his voice level, reasonable.

"You got the wrong man, whoever you are."

"Oh, sure! You're just hiding out here for your health. Stand up, slow, and keep your hands above your head."

Ken deliberately placed the frying pan to one side, half turning his head and catching sight of the man from the corner of his eye. Then he lifted his hands and slowly stood up, just as slowly turned. He looked in blank surprise at the dock foreman, the man with whom he had played poker, who had befriended him.

Ken blurted, "Hal! What kind of talk—"

"Shut up, Ballard. Friend talk won't work after what you done to Lou."

"But I haven't seen Lou since the fight with Sparks!"

The foreman's twisted mouth showed his disbelief. "You were seen near where he was killed."

"That's crazy! I left Sioux Springs yesterday morning and rode direct here last night. No one's seen me, and I have no idea where Lou Hanes was killed."

"Three witnesses heard the shot and saw you riding away. They found Lou, and they found a neckerchief you probably wore as a mask in case your bushwhack went wrong. They found a rifle shell."

"Hal, I swear—"

"You swear in court—if you live to get to trial. Folks thought the world of Lou Hanes. Now you stand hitched while I look at your rifle."

Ken's lips flattened; then he saw the uselessness of argument. He settled on his heels, arms still lifted as the foreman moved cautiously forward to the bedroll and the leather scabbard. He pulled the weapon out, slanted a look at Ken, some distance away.

Ken said, "That gun hasn't been fired since I bought it."

"Maybe, but I'll look anyhow."

The foreman held the rifle at the ready, jerked the mechanism and a bullet jumped out. He picked it up with grim satisfaction. "Same kind of load as the cartridge they found."

Ken answered patiently, "I reckon there's a hundred rifles in the county that'd fire the same kind of shell. Look down the bore."

"I'll do that."

The man moved far back to the edge of the clearing. He knelt down and placed his Colt beside him on the ground where he could sweep it up and fire before Ken could cover half the distance

144

between them. Giving Ken a long, hard, warning look, he opened the rifle breach, reversed the weapon, and peered down the muzzle. Ken waited patiently.

The rifle lowered, the foreman's voice came, tight. "Were you running a bluff, Ballard? This rifle's been fired—recently. Were you so hell bent to escape after the murder that you forgot?"

Ken stared. "It can't be! I haven't used that gun, I tell you!"

The foreman picked up his Colt and rose, tucking the rifle under his arm. "Liar! I can see. And so will the sheriff. Along with the neckerchief—"

"What neckerchief?"

"Now don't tell me you don't have a neckerchief!"

"Sure, I have half a dozen there in my bedroll, besides the one I'm wearing."

"Okay, you open the roll and spread 'em out. And don't think I won't pull this trigger."

Ken lowered his arms and moved to the bedroll. He opened it, pushed the socks and underwear aside, and counted the neckerchiefs in the small pile, spreading them out. He looked up, his face stricken and drawn.

"Four!" the foreman said angrily. "You said six. Four there, you're wearing one, and there's another in the sheriff's office. Sam Loo, the laundryman, put his hentrack marks on it, and he knew it was yours the minute the sheriff showed him."

"But it can't be!" Ken said in a stricken, far-off voice.

The foreman didn't bother to argue any further. He indicated the clothing and the blankets. "Roll 'em and tie 'em, Ballard. You got a date with the sheriff—and a hemp rope."

"But, Hal—"

"Shut up, before I think too much about the bullet in Lou's back."

Ken saw the uselessness of argument or further protest. He replaced the clothing, moving slowly, despite the foreman's impatience, thinking, gauging his chances. Certain of the authority of the Colt in his hand, the foreman moved closer.

Ken judged the distance with an under-brow glance. He rolled the blanket and then moved carefully to the fire. He smothered it, kicking dirt upon the embers, emptied the coffee pot and turned to the frying pan he had set to one side.

The foreman moved closer, eyes narrowed and watchful. Ken bent to the skillet, where the bacon lay still crisp and the grease bubbled with heat. He grasped the handle, saw the foreman throw a glance over toward the horse.

Ken straightened in a flash, swinging around, and the skillet sailed straight and hard toward the foreman's head. Its hot contents spewed out.

The foreman caught a glimpse of it, threw up his arm to ward it off.

Ken took a lunging stride and made a long dive for the foreman's legs. The man struck the skillet aside but grimaced in pain as some of the hot grease struck his hand and cheek. He half turned, his gun lifting.

Ken struck his legs just as the gun exploded, the bullet whipping harmlessly over Ken's head. His arms wrapped desperately around the legs and the catapulting force of his body tipped the foreman over and down. The two men fell in a mad threshing of legs and arms.

They struck the ground with a jarring thud. Ken's hand darted for the foreman's gun wrist and his fingers wrapped around the arm. His muscles bunched as he forced the arm back so that the Colt could not come into play. The foreman struck blindly at him and his fist rapped on Ken's skull, bring momentary flashes of light.

Ken hung on grimly. He brought his knee up in a jolting blow into Hal's stomach. The foreman's breath expelled in a painful grunt, his mouth gaping and his eyes distended. For a moment his long jaw was exposed and Ken's fist pistoned against its point. The foreman dropped back as though poleaxed, his fingers spasmodically opening. The gun fell free. Ken vaulted the limp body, grabbed the weapon, and whipped about, leveling it.

The foreman lay unmoving, eyes closed, body

slack. Ken breathed hard for a moment, then looked searchingly about. He saw the shadowy shape of the foreman's horse back in the trees. After a quick glance at the unconscious man, he raced to the animal.

He returned in a moment with a coil of rope retrieved from the saddle. Working swiftly, he trussed the man in his own rope. Then Ken sank back on his heels, expelling his breath in a deep sigh of relief. The foreman still lay with eyes closed, the coils of rope lashing his arms to his sides, his hands behind his back.

Ken went to the stream and filled the coffee pot with water. He returned and poured it on his captive's face. The man gasped and his eyes fluttered open. They focused on Ken and he tried to jump up, but fell back. Then he looked frightened, though he tried to hide it as Ken knelt beside him.

"Sorry to do this to you, Hal, but I had to. You wouldn't listen to me."

The foreman moistened his lips. "I reckon you'll kill me now."

"I never killed anyone," Ken nearly shouted, then gained control of his anger. "You bowled me over with the news about Hanes. And then to say that I done it—"

"The signs point right at you."

"Maybe, but I didn't do it. Hal, where was Lou killed?"

"North of town. He was heading out to that station you made on your first run. That's why you knew a good place to—"

"Leave me out of it. I was never there." Ken glared as the foreman's eyes shifted away. "Go ahead. How did it happen?"

"Well, you—that is, someone, waited where the road cuts through low hills. Sign looks like he waited a long time—droppings, tracks, things like that. Frank Sparks and the sheriff figure you—someone—saw Lou leave and made a fast circle ride to meet him there. Looks like they talked and then Lou rode on. Then—someone—pulled out his rifle and shot Lou in the back."

Ken waited a moment for the man to continue. When he didn't, Ken asked, "And my neckerchief was found there?"

"No, the spent cartridge. Sparks and the sheriff trailed you—" The foreman checked, then continued when Ken did not react. "The killer cut off the road and headed west. They found the neckerchief about half a mile away."

Ken shook his head. "Do you think I'd go to the trouble of waylaying and murdering a man and then be fool enough to leave something that'd point right to me? Why should I drop a neckerchief? It don't make sense!"

The captive frowned, then his lips curled. "I don't know why. Point is, you were seen—by three witnesses."

"Who?"

"Chuckline riders who happened to be up that way. Said they'd seen you before in town and so they recognized you up there. They said you rode by hell for leather and didn't even see 'em. By then you were heading south."

Ken threw his arms wide in futile amazement. "It's impossible! The hostler can tell you—"

"He did, and he said that you headed south. But there was time for you to circle north. Sparks is damn sure that's what you did, and those riders identified you."

Ken crouched down beside the foreman. "Who were those men?"

"Just drifters. One I've seen around town, at the saloon. Gave his name as Scatlin."

"Scatlin!"

Ken sank back on his heels, trying to fit the pieces into a logical, believable picture. Scatlin— Nixon's man and therefore on Brad Moran's payroll. He began to get the picture then and he felt a chill of nerves along his back.

"Where is Scatlin?"

"With the posse—him and his two friends."

Ken jerked to his feet. "With the posse! Deputized?" He felt the chill again when the foreman nodded. "They'll shoot at the first sight of me."

"So will Frank," the foreman snapped and then realized he might have angered a dangerous man. "He's sure you did it, Ballard. You and him fought and then Hanes backed him up when he fired you. It all figures, the way he sees it."

"The way anyone would see it!"

Ken moved distractedly to the dead fire, thinking furiously. He had been deliberately marked as a killer, the backshooter of a man well respected throughout this whole country. Not only Sparks, but almost any man, would shoot him on sight. Suddenly he wheeled about. If the foreman, a part of the posse, had stumbled onto him, then—

"Where's the sheriff?" Ken demanded.

"The posse's scouring the woods."

Ken moved quickly. He swept up his saddle roll, slid the incriminating rifle into the scabbard and attached it to the saddle of his horse. He returned to the trussed man, who shrank away from him slightly. He loosened the rope enough to get slack to work down to the man's legs and lash them firmly. Then he stood up and surveyed the job.

"I'm going to leave you, Hal. It'll take you two-three hours to work your way to the road. Someone will come along sooner or later. By then I'll be well on the way to Pass City and points beyond."

He turned away, then swung back. "Tell the sheriff, Frank Sparks—all of them—that I didn't kill Lou Hanes."

He met the frightened but disbelieving eyes and then turned away again, swung into saddle and rode slowly into the trees. Reaching the foreman's horse, he gathered up the dangling reins and rode on. He looked back toward his campsite and could no longer see it. He wondered how the foreman had found it, then noticed that the breeze blew from the creek toward the road. The wind could have carried the aroma of wood smoke and sizzling bacon.

Ken felt thankful that the foreman had been alone. Now he had a chance. Just ahead he could see the road through the trees and he turned north, paralleling it. If he should be tracked after his captive was found, this would support his deliberate statement about heading over the mountains to Pass City.

He rode cautiously, ears strained for any sound, eyes constantly probing through the trees. The way grew rough, the ground sloping sharply up toward the first rise of the Treacheries. Now he was to one side and above the road through the pass. Once, when the trees thinned, he saw a portion of the trail below, a yellow curve of dust.

He froze as four armed riders appeared around a bend. Looking down on them as they rode grimly along, with the sun glinting on the badges on their shirts, he eased the rifle out of its scabbard and waited tensely. He was exposed, but they had not looked up. Any movement would call their attention to him.

The dragging seconds passed and then the riders disappeared around the curve and into the trees. Ken discovered that a light sweat covered his forehead. He replaced the rifle and moved higher into the broken country, now working away from the road.

Some distance further along he felt it was safe to release the foreman's horse. It would head for the station directly across country. Free of the animal, Ken rode faster until he drew rein in an isolated canyon. Here, at least, he felt temporarily safe from the vengeful posse and could have time to think.

He needed that time, and he needed to think clearly. If he failed, he could die from a lawman's bullet.

XII

Ken dismounted, ground tying the horse for the rest it needed after the hard and grueling ride. He dropped on a fallen log, looking at the animal but not really seeing it. His mind picked up pictures from the past, and now he could understand their deadly significance.

He saw the bartender at Pass City who told of Brad Moran's failure to move in on Lou Hanes or even to invade his territory profitably. Ken recalled now there had even been an attempt at raiding, but it was swiftly broken up and some of the men were killed because of Sparks' swift action. So Brad Moran had been blocked at every legal turn, and even the illegal ways.

Except one, Ken thought—murder. That was what Moran had had in mind from the beginning. With Hanes dead, Moran would figure his daughter could not hold the business together. Moran would move in then, or wreck and raid, driving the girl to the wall. So long as the murder could not be pinned on Moran, he stood a good chance to get all the business north of Treachery.

Ken saw now that everything that had happened to him made sense. Moran needed a killer, someone completely unknown and in no way connected with him. Who better than a wandering hobo? As Moran had said time and again, no one cared if a bum's body was found with a bullet in it, or if he disappeared.

Perhaps Moran had hoped to find someone who'd actually pull the trigger for a price. However, in Ken he had settled for second best, a man who could be cleaned up, trained as a freightwagon driver, placed in Hanes' organization. So Moran had risked one more raid on the Hanes wagons, not to destroy but to eliminate a driver so Ken could take the job.

Ken suddenly laughed without mirth. He had felt bad about being a spy! How did it feel to be a killer, in the eyes of the law? Those fake visits of Nixon's, asking how many wagons worked the routes and the amount of the business! Ken himself had not seen the sense of it, but now it seemed like clear-cut logic: keep Ken looking in one direction while a trap was set in another!

But how had they sprung it? Ken paced back and forth, frowning. Moran had played in luck all along. Sparks' pride and jealousy had helped. Alice Hanes had persuaded her father to promote Ken, and that brought Sparks' antagonism to a head. More luck for Moran! And when Ken reported it, Moran and Nixon had been ready to move in and wait for the inevitable explosion. With what a fine show of regret Moran had accepted the fact that Ken might be fired! Again Ken grimaced, wondering how he could have

155

been such a fool. He had himself deliberately brought on that firing—thinking to fool Moran!

Ken shrugged these bitter self-recriminations aside. It was done now, neatly done, just as the fired rifle, the spent shell, and the neckerchief had been used. Ken stopped short, suddenly realizing how Nixon had boxed him in and set him up. Scatlin coming to the hotel and the night ride to meet Nixon. Then Scatlin had left—going right back to the hotel and Ken's room. Simple to take a neckerchief from the pile in the drawer. Simple to take the rifle, race beyond the town, fire it and return it to the closet.

All the while Nixon held Ken with talk of Brad Moran's fairness. Ken had wages coming, unexpected wages. All he had to do was start out the next morning for Pass City and collect. He had been practically ordered to and, like a fool, the lure of the wages had sent Ken south the next day.

From that moment, Lou Hanes was dead. They had only to watch and wait for the right time and place. Not even that—if Nixon figured time pressed, Haines could have been killed at his home, the office. Because Ken Ballard must be tied in to the murder.

Ken swung around, feeling the crawl of nerves as the extent of the trap became clear. Who had killed Hanes? Scatlin? Who then moved out with his friends and waited for the right time to lie about seeing Ken? Had Nixon done the killing himself, leaving the other three to play their deadly roles?

Ken strode to the horse, checked the rifle loading, pulled a new cartridge belt and a holstered Colt from the bedroll and strapped them on. Moran's gift, he thought in deadly anger, part of the masquerade. He checked the chambers, slid the weapon back in the holster with the feeling that the Colt itself might be part of the trickery. He looked about, glimpsing the high peaks through the trees. The wilderness silence was broken only by the sigh of the wind far above.

He faced a choice. He could run, could work his way west or east through this mountain country and have a fair chance of escape. But he knew the ways of the law and knew that from this moment on he would always be the target for a bounty hunter's gun, or a sheriff in some far-off town who had read the wanted dodgers. There would be no rest.

Guilt—his flight would be proof of that, in everyone's eyes. He would never know peace or security again. He thought of the dreams and plans of a new life he had so recently made. All that would now go by the board.

His second choice made his eyes grow bleak and his mouth grim. Nixon or Scatlin had pulled the trigger. Only they knew the truth—they and Brad Moran. But Ken knew that the man could claim ignorance of the killing and make it stick. He was probably in Pass City and could prove he had never left.

So it was Scatlin or Nixon. He had to find one or both, and that meant he must ride back to Sioux Springs, right into the jaws of danger. Scatlin and his gunhawks rode with the posse. Their bullets would cut him down before he could talk. Nixon would probably shoot on sight. That would be true of Frank Sparks, too. He enlarged on the thought. It would be true of everybody.

But he had to risk it if he wanted to walk free again—and that he very much wanted to do. Then he suddenly realized that he wanted Alice Hanes to know he had not murdered her father. There had been a spark between them, an interest and a warmth, the first Ken had known in years. The ghost of Carla Wayne had forced him to reject a growing friendship, but he knew now that this had been wrong.

Ken looked southward, hesitated a moment, and then gathered the reins and swung into saddle. A touch of the spurs and he moved cautiously down the canyon, his right hand never far from his Colt, his eyes and ears alert.

The sun stood at meridian when he broke through to the southern descending slope. He had worked eastward again and knew that the road must be a short distance off through the trees to his right. A few miles straight ahead the mountains would melt into the rolling open range.

He lifted the reins and then froze, catching the sound of a voice not far off. He backed the horse behind bushes, swung out of saddle and grasped the animal's muzzle. His right hand slid the Colt from the holster and he dogged back the trigger. Tense and unmoving, he waited.

A moment later, three armed riders moved between trees off to his right. They came on and Ken, eyes narrowed, half raised the Colt. The men came closer. He didn't know them but he saw the badges on their shirts.

They halted, bunched, and one looked directly up the slope at the bushes that screened Ken and the horse. The casual glance swept on and then the man turned to the others as they pulled out tobacco sacks and rolled cigarettes.

Ken remained frozen. He could distinctly hear the words as the voices drifted up to him. "I figure Sparks and the sheriff are wasting time. Hal Smith said Ballard was heading for Pass City."

"Maybe Hal heard wrong," one said.

"He's lucky to be hearing at all," the third said. "Damn fool! Running in on a killer like that, all alone!"

Ken felt a slight touch of relief that the foreman had been found. But the men still talked, as they lazed in the saddle and smoked.

"The sheriff figures Ballard said that to throw us off." The voice came clearly. "Chances are he'll keep on this side of the mountains and work his way out of the county. A rider to Pass City took the news to the lawman over there. So our back-shooting friend has two sheriffs looking for him."

"Sparks is sure anxious to put a bullet in him."

"So'm I! Lou Hanes was a hell of a good man in my tally book." The man lifted the reins."Well, let's spread out and look for sign. Remember the signal if you see Ballard or his tracks."

"Two shots and then two more."

"And don't try to close in alone, like Hal Smith done. You might not be so lucky."

The men broke up then, one heading down the slope, one along and across it, the third angling up toward the screen of bushes. Ken's lips tightened as he watched the man approach. His eyes jumped to the others in time to see one disappear off to the left.

The approaching rider circled a tree and continued up the slope at the new angle. It took him far to the left of Ken's hiding place and in a moment he disappeared. The third man had also vanished.

For a time Ken heard faint sounds and then all was silence. He eased out his breath then and gently lowered the hammer on the Colt, sliding it again into the holster. Still, he did not leave the cover, knowing that the three meant that other searchers were close about. They were probably crisscrossing the slope. He gave the sheriff and

Sparks grudging credit. Sending a single rider to alert the law in Pass City enabled the sheriff to cover this side of the mountains.

Almost an hour passed and Ken finally rode carefully down the slope. Every nerve urged him to speed but he knew that his thin margin of safety depended on slow, cautious going. An accidental meeting could mean death immediately, or an exchange of shots that would bring the rest of the posse running.

At last, late in the afternoon, Ken reined in and looked out beyond the last line of trees to the open range. He had the feeling that riding out there would expose him to every gun arrayed against him. Yet he knew there was an equal risk in remaining here on the mountain slopes.

He took a deep breath, touched spurs and rode on. Soon the trees were behind him and he rode tall and clear across the rolling grasslands. He held his horse to a slow steady pace and checked an impulse to look back at the forested mountain slopes. The trees would block the view of the plain from the searchers up there, he knew. If, by chance, one should get a view, Ken would only be a slow-moving speck. At the distance and with this unhurried pace, he would look like a working puncher going unconcernedly about his business.

The distance between him and the mountains widened. He angled for a time toward the road and then headed directly for distant Sioux

Springs. He had no definite plans as yet and could make none. Nixon might easily be in town awaiting developments, word that Ken had been shot down or, at least, captured. He might be in Pass City, reporting to Moran. In either place he would be out of Ken's reach for the time being.

Hank Scatlin rode with the posse somewhere in the mountains. He was also safe. Ken could only keep in hiding near Sioux Springs, wait for a chance at Nixon or the return of the posse and a chance at Scatlin.

A safe distance from keen eyes on the mountain slopes behind him, Ken set a fast pace. He made a few wide circles around ranches to avoid being seen. The miles rolled behind him as the sun sank and the sky began to lose its color. Night caught him still several miles from Sioux Springs.

He pressed on, thinking to circle the town and make a lonely, hidden camp in the hilly country just to the north. No one would think to look for him there. Soon he saw the distant town lights and started his circuit. The lights wheeled slowly to his right and behind him. He then cut directly to the road. It would be safe enough now and he'd avoid a chance gopher hole or arroyo in this open range land.

He hit the road, reined in and looked back toward the cluster of lights. They'd all be talking about him, he thought bitterly, hating him for something he hadn't done. He thought of Alice

Hanes, wondered where she'd be. At the station waiting word that her father had been avenged? At the undertaker's? Or in lonely mourning at the Hanes ranch home just a mile or so down this very road?

She, like all the rest, would think of Ken Ballard as a man who deserved killing, one whom Lou Hanes had tried to help and who had repaid the old man with a bullet. Ken sighed in futile, angry regret and spoke a quiet word to the horse, moving it out into the road. As soon as luck or fate put Hank Scatlin or Tag Nixon in his gunsights, he'd change all that.

Not long after, he came to a ranch road that led toward a distant grove of trees. He could see a faint flicker of light over there as he rode along. Passing the road, he abruptly drew rein and returned the few yards to the dark, small sign. With a searching glance in all directions, he dismounted, struck a match and read the black painted words, "Singletree Ranch—Lou Hanes."

The match burned out and Ken stood looking toward the dark copse of trees. He could not see the light since he had dismounted but he knew that Alice was there, probably alone with her grief. Undoubtedly, he thought, hating Ken Ballard. He bit his lips, indecisive. Logic told him to ride on; some strong inner need urged him to tell her the truth without delay.

He drove away the thought as being too

dangerous. He turned to the horse, swung into saddle, reined about. Find a camp and— He could hear her voice in his mind, could see the smoke-violet eyes. Her tone had tried to be impersonal but she could not keep a warm interest out of it. She had tried to help and he knew that it was more than the sort of kindness she might show to any employee.

He drew rein, twisted about in the saddle. Now he could see the steady, lonely light again, a sad spark almost engulfed in the uncaring expanse of the night. With a curse at his own foolishness, he turned again and this time moved slowly up the ranch road. Strangely, though he might ride into danger, he felt relieved.

He came into the ranch yard and dismounted, eyes darting here and there to the shadows. There had been no challenge but Ken still held his hand close to his gun. Nothing moved in the yard. A single window in the ranch house glowed with lamplight. He swung out of saddle and, moving tensely, drifted to the porch steps.

He tested each step before he trusted his weight to it. None creaked. Edging at an angle across the porch to the window, he looked in. Alice Hanes sat on a horsehair divan, hands folded in her lap, staring dully at the opposite wall. Her eyes looked swollen and, even as Ken looked, her lips quivered and she suddenly buried her face in her hands. No one else was in the room.

Ken felt a surge of sympathy for the lonely girl. He moved to the door. Through the inset of glass he could see the dark hallway, the light streaming into it from the room in which Alice sat. He looked over his shoulder, giving the yard a searching look, then tapped lightly on the door.

He waited, tapped again, saw the girl's shadow and then Alice herself as she came into the hallway. As the door opened he stepped back, and swept off his hat.

She looked out, uncertain of the shadowy figure he formed. "Yes? Who is it?"

"Ma'am, I had to see you."

He stepped into the half light and she gasped, hand lifting to her mouth. He said quickly, "Miss Alice, I didn't shoot your father. No matter what they say, I didn't kill him."

She recovered some control; her hand dropped and her breasts rose and fell raggedly. Her voice came with choked difficulty. "Mr. Ballard, I . . . Please come in."

She turned and walked back toward the lighted room. Ken entered the hall slowly, hat in his hand. Alice reached the lighted doorway, stepped beyond it, then reappeared again, facing him.

The lamplight glinted on the blue steel of the Colt she leveled at Ken. In a split-second, startled look at her tight face, Ken knew she intended to pull the trigger.

XIII

He threw himself to one side against the wall a moment before the gun lanced flame, and thunder filled the narrow confines of the hallway. Glass crashed behind him as the bullet smashed through the door; the strong odor of burned powder filled the room.

His shoulder struck the wall and then he flung himself forward, reaching for the girl and the gun before she could fire it again. She tried to twist away but his fingers taloned into a slim, soft shoulder. Screaming, she tried to bring up the heavy gun.

His hand wrapped around her slender wrist and he twisted her arm aside. For a moment her lovely strained face was close to his, the full lips pulled back from gleaming teeth in a grimace of strain and hate. His fingers tightened on her wrist and the Colt thudded to the floor.

Releasing her, he pushed her aside and bent down to scoop up the fallen weapon. He grabbed it, straightened as she whirled about and raced toward the lighted room. She fled, blindly, and he knew he could not let her get away. He jumped after her, caught her as she raced around a table toward a dark doorway beyond.

The moment his hands touched her, she turned

in blind, fighting fury. Fingers clawed at his face, toes kicked at his shins. He grabbed her wrists but she still kicked. A strand of hair had fallen loose and hung over her shoulder.

Grimly, he forced her back and felt her slender body struggle against him. He pushed her against a wall and held her immobilized. Raging breath panted from her opened lips and he held her forcefully until the fury of her resistance suddenly broke.

Then he cautiously eased the muffling pressure of his body against hers, but held her wrists and arms above and back of her head against the wall. His own breath came raggedly as he spoke.

"Please, Miss Alice, I came to talk to you."

"Talk!" she blazed. "What's there to talk about? Father's dead. Did you come to kill me too?"

"Listen to me, that's all; just listen."

She renewed her effort to escape but her frantic tugging lasted only a moment. Exhausted, she could only glare at him.

"Listen, Miss Alice. You have to give me a chance—"

"I tried to give you what you deserved. Don't give me another chance or—"

His fingers tightened about her wrists and she winced from the pressure. He spoke slowly and tightly. "Miss Alice, a man's got a right to clear himself. That's all I'm asking. Just listen to me. I can tell you while holding you like this, or you can sit down like a lady. It's your choice."

She glared at him but his firm, steady eyes held hers. Finally she looked away and spoke in a bitter, choked voice. "I guess I don't have any choice but to listen to your lies."

"You decide if they're lies or not."

He released her wrists and stepped back. If she made a dart to escape, he could catch her with a single lunging step. She rubbed her wrists, glowering at him. Then she straightened and, with an angry toss of the head, moved slowly to the horsehair sofa.

He moved with her, swung a chair around as she sat down and, being a woman, tried to rearrange her hair. He saw that she wouldn't try to escape, at least for a time, and he sat down in the chair.

"I didn't shoot your—"

"I'm tired of hearing that! I know what happened."

"You only know what you've been told."

Her voice remained ice. "I suppose you have another story. Sorry, I believe my friends and what I've seen."

Doggedly he pushed on. "Miss Alice, would I risk a bullet or a hangrope coming here if I wasn't innocent? I'd be gone far yonderly."

She remained still, arms lifted to her hair as the smoke-violet eyes probed and studied him. He took a deep and ragged breath. "You know nothing about me, where I come from or why I came to Sioux Springs."

"Should I care?" she flared.

"Yes, you should. You'll learn the truth about this shooting. You'll know there's a lot more to come, now that Brad Moran—"

"Moran!"

Now he had her startled attention in full. He told her the whole story, starting with the destruction Carla Wayne had wrought that led to his wanderings, and his kidnapping by Brad Moran. He told her of his training, and Moran's plans, of the deliberate wagontrain raid and Jake Lacey's removal.

He saw a growing contempt for him under her close attention to his story. He flushed and tried to explain—his own attitude, forced on him by life, the threats of Brad Moran and Tag Nixon. Both had trapped and held him. He told her of his scheme to escape the situation by getting himself fired.

"So that's why you had the fight!" she breathed.

"Yes, ma'am, that's why. But it only played right into Moran's hands."

Then he told her the rest of the story, of his near capture and his escape. He told her of his determination to clear himself and his return to Sioux Springs.

"I'm crazy to be here," he ended. "I should've waited until I could get to Scatlin or Nixon. But there's a good chance I won't make it—too many guns waiting for me out there. So I wanted you to know, even if I can't prove it yet."

Abruptly he stood up, paced, almost forgetting the girl. "Six months ago, I wouldn't have cared what anyone thought about me. Even yesterday, maybe, for I figured a man needs pride and confidence only in himself. Then, this morning, I find I'm branded a killer and an outlaw. I knew you believed I'd murdered your father and men I've known and worked with—like Hal Smith— mark me as a sneaking, dangerous sidewinder."

He turned, looking down at her; he had all her attention now. "So I knew a man's belief in himself is not enough. It's a lot, a mighty lot, but not enough. He can't be rock bottom sure of himself until he sees that others are sure of him, that they see him as he sees himself."

He shook his head, trying to clarify his thoughts, and took a few more paces, then whirled and looked down at her again. "Maybe that's not clear to you. Maybe I'm not saying it like I feel it myself. Point is, I couldn't risk you not knowing my side of the story, knowing I didn't do a yellow bushwhack. Proof will come later, if I'm lucky. But at least I've told you."

She shook her head. "This whole thing's incredible! I know Moran is a ruthless man, but that he'd go to these lengths!"

"He did. I'm right in the middle because of it."

She studied him again. "Do you expect me to believe this?"

He hesitated and then lifted his shoulders, let them fall. "I'd like you to, but I don't expect you to until I can get to Scatlin or Nixon, if you give me that chance."

She laughed, a harsh, tearing sound. "What else can I do? I'm alone with you and—"

"Not that kind of a chance," he cut in. "I'll ride out in a minute. You can do what you please then. Town's close and not every man rode with the sheriff's posse. There'll be enough left so you could have 'em gunning for me in an hour."

"I should."

"Yes, *if* you don't believe me—and I'm not asking you to. I'm just asking you to think I just might be framed for this killing and I need the chance to clear myself. Figure I wouldn't risk coming to you like this if that wasn't so."

He paused, watching her. She looked down at the floor now, shoulders bent. He started to speak, changed his mind and walked to the hallway. Seeing the big Colt lying on the floor where he had dropped it to race after her and stop her flight, he bent down, picked it up, and returned again to the room.

She looked up and saw the gun in his hand, and a new fear rushed into her eyes. He placed the weapon on the table. "It's yours. Use it if you want to."

He turned away again and strode down the dark hallway. He jerked open the door with the bullet-shattered glass and stepped out on the porch. In a moment he had crossed it and walked to his horse. He heard no sound behind him and he did not look back.

There was a crawling sensation along his back, but he disregarded it. He swung into saddle, lifted the reins and then saw Alice Hanes' figure silhouetted on the porch by the light streaming from the open door behind her. His hesitation lasted but a second.

He reined the horse about and rode slowly away, back toward the main highway. Again he felt that uncertain crawling along his back. He had caught the faint glint of the gun the girl had held at her side, partially concealed by her skirt. But he reached the yard fence and rode on in a strange, tense silence.

Dawn found Ken threading the swales between low hills east of Sioux Springs. He knew that he had left a very confused girl at the Hanes ranch and that she could as easily raise an alarm as she could keep silence. If she did race to town with the news of his presence, the searchers would comb northward. Playing safe, Ken had made a second circuit of the town and now looked for some place where he could gain needed rest to prepare for the ordeal ahead.

He felt amazed at the speed with which he had developed the keen senses of the hunted. Now his eyes constantly searched bush, tree, slope of hill, dip of swale. His ears keened to the wind for the faintest sound of pursuit. Tired as he was, his brain worked swiftly, planning and weighing.

His problem was to remain close to the town so that he would know when the sheriff tired of combing the mountains and came back with the main posse. Also he had to plan on a second group of trackers roused by Alice Hanes, and avoid them. Even if she had not spread the alarm, Ken must find a hideout to avoid a chance encounter with punchers working the range. Recognition by anyone would bring the wolves of the law howling down on him.

So he rode slowly and cautiously, ready for trouble at any moment. Midmorning found him deep in the broken hill country. None of the hills were high and most were bare of everything but stirrup-tall grass. But they offered cover and that, for the moment, was all he asked.

He rounded the base of a hill and drew rein, looking out into a small meadow snugged between the knolls. On the far side he saw a low, squat structure, a line shack. His eyes moved sharply about the valley, saw no sign of life. With hand close to his holster, Ken rode across the meadow toward the shack.

The door was closed, the single window dusty.

Coming closer, Ken saw that the grass about the doorway was untrampled. The place looked as if it hadn't been used in months. He drew rein and looked around at the protecting hills with satisfaction. Deserted, or seldom used, and close enough to town, the shack made a perfect hiding place. He rode around the structure. A small grassy area in the rear between the shack and the abrupt, broken wall of the hill behind would make a hiding place for the horse.

In half an hour Ken sat within the shack, cooking, on the rusty stove, his first meal in almost two days. Later, he spread his bedroll o an ancient bunk, braced a chair against the door. He dropped on the bunk and went to sleep, his gun in his hand.

It was late afternoon when he awoke. He scouted the meadow and the hills from the dusty window, then went out to check his horse. He brought more water from a small well beyond the shack and cooked supper, had coffee. By then the twilight had come, but he welcomed it.

With full night he saddled up and rode out. He headed directly for the town and within two hours saw its distant lights. He drifted toward them, keeping away from the roads. It was taking a long chance, he knew, but he had to know when the posse returned or if there were signs that a second, aroused by Alice Hanes, might be searching for him.

He drifted to the road that would give him a view down the short main street. Everything looked peaceful; the hitchracks were bare and deserted. He glanced at the nearest houses, dark this late at night, and then he moved deeper into the town. Darkness covered him and the street was empty but he still ran a risk. He started when a dog suddenly barked from within one of the dark houses, but he moved on. Soon he could see the sheriff's office, as dark as the houses. So, he thought—the posse had not yet returned and he would have to wait another day, maybe two.

He looked ahead at the lights from the nearby saloon, the hotel and the livery beyond, the second saloon on the opposite side of the street. There was no activity that he could see, and this confirmed the absence of most of the men.

He neck reined the horse about and moved back the way he had come. Again the dark houses and once more the muffled barking. He silently cursed the dog. If anyone looked out the window and saw him! Then he realized he would appear to be a late rider returning to one of the ranches. No one would expect Lou Hanes' killer to be riding boldly in Sioux Springs.

But he couldn't do this often. He wished that he could find a hiding place closer than the line shack. Suddenly he drew rein, the memory galvanizing him. The deserted and disintegrating house he had often noticed at the northern edge of town! He moved on and, clear of the last buildings, made a swift wide circuit of the town.

Again he moved cautiously in, this time from the north along the very road the returning posse would use. He saw the dark, squat shape of the structure he sought just ahead. It stood alone in a tangle of ragged grass and weeds. Ken left the road and came into the place from the rear. His eyes lighted when he saw the canted shape of an ancient shed, perfect for his horse. With a look toward the sleeping town, he moved in, swung out of saddle and crept forward to investigate. When he found the place to be as deserted as it looked from the outside, he knew he had discovered an ideal hiding place.

He spent the greater part of the night riding, back to the line shack where he collected his few belongings, then a return journey to the abandoned house. He let the horse graze on a picket rope during the dark, silent hours that remained before daylight. Then he went to the house and braced the sagging-open front door, using a wedge to keep it from swinging fully back.

When it began to get light he brought the horse to the ancient shed and then sought his own hiding place. Afterward he lay down for an hour or two of sleep. He awakened to the sound of a buckboard rattling by in the bright morning, and took a position beside a dirt-clouded front window from which he could watch the road.

Hours passed. He saw two Hanes freight wagons, heavy loaded, roll by. A carriage passed, ranch wagons, a buckboard, two riders. No one so much as glanced at the ancient house, and Ken grimly wondered what they would do if they knew a hunted man watched them. The sun moved higher and Ken kept his post. Now and then he moved about the room to relieve cramped muscles, but always he returned to the window.

He grew hungry but knew he must wait until total darkness, when the last-chance riders had left the saloons and the town had gone to bed. Mentally he checked his dwindling food supply and knew he could last another day, maybe two if he tightened his belt.

The sun moved westerly and now the shadow of the shack extended out toward the road. Traffic lessened, then stopped altogether. Ken stood up stiffly and stretched, knowing the wait had been fruitless. Arms at full length above his head, he suddenly stiffened at a faint sound.

He jumped to the window and peered out through the splay of black spiderwebs, the patina of dust. The sounds grew louder—many riders. Ken's fingers tightened on the dirty window sill.

Then he saw them out there on the road. First the sheriff, with Frank Sparks beside him. They rode wearily, as men do whose efforts have been unrewarded. Ken's eyes flicked to the riders who followed, at least fifty men. He had a wry sense of his own importance that so many men had been called to hunt him down. That passed and his attention centered on the riders.

He saw the foreman, and felt relieved as though he had placed the man in danger. His eyes cast along each face as the riders passed.

Then his knuckles grew white with the pressure of his fingers on the sill. The pinched face, the heavy gunbelt, the careless slouch in the saddle— it was Hank Scatlin, a cigarette dangling from the corner of his lip, waggling as he spoke to the man beside him.

Ken's head turned as the posse passed. He stood up slowly as the dust cloud dispersed on the road, and his hand half lifted, formed into a fist and then dropped to the Colt in his holster.

XIV

As Ken waited for full darkness, the deadly enormity of his task hit him full force. True, the posse had returned and by now would be scattering to the homes of the members or the saloons. Sparks would check at the station first, if Ken knew him, and then go out to the Hanes ranch. Ken wondered momentarily if Alice would tell Frank about him.

But the thought did not linger. His attention centered on Scatlin. Where would he go? Ken would bet one of the saloons would see him. And then? Did Scatlin stay at the hotel? Or somewhere else in town? Wherever he stayed, it was a place where Ken hardly dared go if he wanted to live. But he must if he wanted to wring the truth from the gundog.

Ken checked his Colt, watched the twilight deepen into night. When only the stars gave light, he left the shack, flitting out the door like a phantom. He did not go near the road but moved at an angle that would take him to the rear of the buildings along the main street. His plans were vague; they had to be. Good luck—or bad—would be the deciding factor anyway. He would have to act as opportunity or disaster dictated.

Scatlin and his renegade friends would most

likely remain in town tonight, probably at one of the saloons. They would be wearied from their fruitless days on the mountains, and they wouldn't want to make any suspicious move in an attempt to reach Nixon or Moran. They held all the cards, so they'd be satisfied. Thus, tonight would be Ken's best chance, slim as it was—before the gunhawks slipped away.

He heard faint stompings in the livery stable as he ghosted along the rear of the structure. Ahead, the alley, a shallow canyon between low buildings and squat sheds, gave a dark but uncertain haven for his movements. He could hear faint sounds from the street beyond.

He moved on, passing the hardware store, then stopped short at the narrow dark passage between it and the saddlery. He could see the street, caught the flare of a match as a man on the walk paused to light a cigarette. The man moved on and Ken poised, uncertain. Then he eased into the narrow passageway.

He edged along it and stopped several feet short of the street. A rider went by, and then loud footsteps sounded. Two men passed; he caught a few words of their conversation.

". . . bury Lou Hanes in the morning. Too bad Ballard won't be hanging somewhere."

"He's long gone from here. But give it time. Sooner or later . . ."

The voices faded as the men moved beyond

earshot. Ken, flattened against the wall, felt a grim clutch of prophetic fear that he choked down. He had one shred of news but realized that he must have a vantage place closer to the saloon where Scatlin would most likely be. He crept back down the passageway and once more along the alley.

Moving slowly along the dark buildings, he grew tense as he approached the rear of the jail and the sheriff's office. There were no lights back here, but he caught the glow from a window up front. He hesitated, weighing the risk, then decided it was no more here than anywhere else in town. His advantage lay in that no one expected him to be around.

He took his time in the slow advance along the side of the jail to a place beside the open window, where he flattened against the building. Lamp-light glowed out to one side and slightly above him. He strained for sound but none came, yet he sensed that someone was inside. Steps suddenly sounded on the low wooden porch to the front of the building, out of his sight.

The sheriff's voice seemed to explode through the window. "Well, Frank, I thought you'd be taking a rest after all that riding."

"No time. With Lou dead and most of us out chasing Ballard, the shipments fell way behind."

"I wish we'd caught him," the sheriff sighed. "How's Miss Alice?"

There was a second's hesitation before Sparks'

voice sounded. "Holding up, but nervous. She stayed out at the ranch all alone instead of having someone stay with her. She shot the glass out of the front door."

"What!"

"Thought she saw or heard someone." Sparks' sigh came clearly to Ken. "She's all broke up and jumpy. Said she thought maybe Ballard had come back."

"Not him!" the lawman snorted. "By the way, those three drifters—Scatlin, Crane and Tomlin—we better see they don't leave town for a couple of months anyhow. Maybe you could use 'em at the station."

"Those bums! Why?"

"Figure it, Frank. Suppose Ballard is picked up somewhere and I bring him back for trial. What's the evidence against him?"

"Hell! Everything!"

"Oh no, it ain't. There's an empty shell of the same caliber as his rifle. How many guns like that are there around? There's the fight with you, and Lou firing him—motive, maybe, but enough to back-shoot? There's the neckerchief. Only thing puts him right close to Lou are those three saddlebums. They saw him. If they drift off we got a mighty weak case when Ballard comes to trial."

"There's a chance he won't," Sparks said grimly, "even if he's caught."

"Forget that talk, Frank! If I bring him in, he

goes to trial or I go down fighting to keep him from a lynch mob."

"All right," Sparks answered grudgingly. "But I can't use those drifters. They're all three across the street right now drinking rotgut until it's coming out their ears. Let someone else hire 'em."

"Well, I'll figure some way to hold 'em," the lawman said patiently.

"See you at the funeral tomorrow?" Sparks asked.

"Lou Hanes is worth any man's last respects, Frank. I'll be there."

Ken heard the hollow steps on the porch again, swiftly gone. Slowly he straightened and carefully worked away from the window. Clear of the building and back in the alley again, he felt a mounting excitement. Alice had not told about him. She had given him that chance! And he knew where Scatlin was.

He adjusted his gunbelt and moved quickly down the alley. North of the short business district, he drifted to the street. A quick look up and down showed no one close. He crossed the street with long hurried strides and the shadows again swallowed him.

A few moments later he drifted to the saloon. He could hear muffled noises through the thin walls as he drifted up toward the rear of the building. He froze when a rear door suddenly opened, a band of light streamed out, and the sound of voices boomed. The light just missed him.

An aproned figure carried a small cask and dropped it with a hollow sound on the loading platform. Ken could hear the man's grunt as he went inside and bent to lift a full keg. He saw the man carry the keg into the barroom. The door remained open, light and noise streaming into the alley.

Ken let his breath out with a shuddering sigh of relief. He threw a look back over his shoulder, then at the open door, and finally eased the Colt from the holster and with several long strides reached the edge of the loading platform. He dropped below it, strained to hear the sounds of approaching feet. Then he removed his hat and slowly lifted himself so that his eyes cleared the platform.

He could look directly into the big room. A corner of the bar cut his vision, but he could see many of the crowded tables. As he looked, a man came to the edge of the bar and signaled for a drink. He slouched against it and turned his head as another man came up.

Ken's eyes glittered. Scatlin! He dropped below the edge of the platform and considered the dark alley, his brain moving fast. The hotel was beyond this saloon, several doors down, and the renegade would probably be staying there. Ken scuttled away from the rear platform at a crouch, avoiding the light that streamed above him.

Shortly thereafter, he eased to the corner beside

the hotel porch, a high structure that cut off the light from the street. The next building was so close from here that he could reach out and touch it. Hearing no sound from the porch or from within the hotel, he risked a peek over the edge of the porch between the rails of the balustrade. There was a line of empty chairs, and nothing else.

He had stayed at this hotel and he visualized the layout of the building, the upper hallways. A glance at the street showed no one near. He jumped, cat-footed, up on the edge of the porch, swung his legs over the balustrade, moved like a shadow to the open door, and peered inside.

An empty lobby, no one at the desk. Beyond it, a door, barely cracked. The night clerk slept there, Ken knew, and the chances were the old man would be doing that right now. Ken silently whirled inside the door, dropped to a crouch as he snaked the Colt from holster. Keeping an eye on the counter, he scuttled across the small lobby and gained the stairway.

The upper hall was dimly lit by a single lamp, the wick turned low. All the doors were closed and Ken involuntarily glanced at the room he had occupied. Silent steps brought him to a narrow door that he jerked open. He stepped into the small broom closet and pulled the door nearly shut. A narrow crack gave him air, admitted sound and enabled him to see a short length of the hallway.

His cramped, strained body felt as though

hours had passed before he heard distant voices and then stumbling steps on the stairs. He stiffened to attention as the boots rapped along the hallway, approached the closet.

"Hank, when we gonta see Tag?"

"Shut up!" a second voice snapped.

"Just askin,' Hank."

"Then ask tomorrow, you loco drunk."

Steps again and then, through the narrow crack, Ken saw Scatlin stop at a door across the hall. Two men blocked his view of the renegade momentarily and then they continued down the hall. Ken heard doors open and slam, saw Scatlin disappear into his room and the door close. Checking an impulse to move now, Ken waited.

He judged when fifteen minutes had passed and then counted a little further. There was no sound now as he eased open the door and stepped into the hall, empty except for himself. A stride took him to Scatlin's door. Colt leveled, he tapped lightly, waited, tapped again.

"Go way!" said a muffled voice.

"Scatlin, open up. Tag wants you."

He heard scuffling sounds and flattened himself against the wall beside the door. It opened slowly, and Scatlin, tousle-haired and sleepy, stepped out. Ken's gun barrel caught him neatly behind the ear and the man fell slack into Ken's arms.

He pulled Scatlin into the room, closed the door. Crossing the shadowy space to the window, he pulled down the blind. Then he struck a match, saw the lamp and lit it.

He turned to Scatlin, who lay unmoving on the floor near the door, where Ken had dropped him. Scatlin wore only long underwear and a pair of socks with a hole in one toe. Ken looked quickly around, then worked swiftly, ripping the bedsheet and tying Scatlin's hands. A portion of the sheet became a gag and another part lashed the man's ankles. Scatlin moaned and Ken used the gun barrel again.

He blew out the lamp, opened the door and looked out into the vacant hallway. Returning, he worked the unconscious man up over his shoulders, balanced the weight and then, gun in his free hand, returned to the hall. There was a back stairway and Ken headed for it and went down. A simple bolt barred the rear door. In a moment, Ken stepped out into the dark alley with his burden.

Some distance down the alley, he had to rest. He eased the bound man to the ground and straightened, breathing deeply. Silence held the sleeping town, for by now even the saloons had closed. Scatlin moved and made mumbling sounds.

Ken bent to him. Scatlin peered into the gray blur of Ken's face and then recognized him. He tried violently to move himself away, but Ken's fingers taloned into his shoulder and Scatlin became rigidly still.

Ken shoved the gun barrel under the man's eyes. "I don't lose a thing if I kill you. Just keep remembering that you put a hangnoose around my neck and I know it. I'm going to untie your feet. Don't try anything."

Ken loosened the knots and jerked Scatlin to his feet. He gestured forward in the darkness and the renegade took a couple of steps, suddenly danced as his stockinged feet struck a stone.

It was long past midnight when they reached the deserted shack on the edge of town. Once inside its dark walls, Ken felt safer, but he also knew his security wouldn't last. When Scatlin turned up missing, with his clothing, boots, and gun still in his room, there'd be a search. It would fan out and sooner or later this refuge would be discovered.

There was nothing for it but flight with this prisoner whose word might absolve Ken of the charge of murder. He forced Scatlin to the shed and saddled his horse. He made the renegade mount and then swung up behind him. A few moments later they rode out of town, heading again for the abandoned line shack in the hills.

Ken awakened when the first bright rays of the sun shone through the dusty window into his eyes. At first he looked blankly about; then sleep left his brain in a rush. He swung out of the bunk and looked down on Scatlin, tightly bound and gagged again, lying on the floor. The pinched eyes glared malevolently at him.

Ken looked out the dusty window onto the little meadow, the silent hills. Satisfied, he turned to his prisoner and forced Scatlin to sit up. He removed the gag and untied the ankles, where rope had been substituted for the twists of ripped sheets. The renegade stomped his feet to restore circuation.

Ken moved to the ancient stove, started a fire and placed the coffee pot on it. He looked over his shoulder at the shivering figure on the floor, ludicrous in dirty long underwear and socks. "You get a cup of coffee to warm you up, Scatlin. Then we'll talk about Lou Hanes."

The man glared. "What's there to talk about?"

"Why you killed him."

Scatlin grunted contemptuously. "You stack up as the bushwhacker, not me."

"You forget, I know I'm not. Did Nixon order you and your two friends to back-shoot Hanes?"

"Whyn't you ask Tag?"

"I'm asking you—and you're going to answer."

Scatlin's eyebrows rose. "What makes you think I will?"

Ken touched his holstered gun. "A Colt, if nothing else will work. What have I got to lose? On the other hand, you ask yourself the same question before we get down to business."

He smiled pleasantly into the suddenly fearful face, then turned to making the coffee.

XV

Gun in one hand, Ken untied Scatlin's wrists and then moved across the room to the bunk. The renegade rubbed his hands to restore circulation and then picked up the tin cup of steaming coffee. He drank it gratefully, and gradually the night cold left his body. With restored warmth came fresh confidence.

"Ballard, you're on the wrong trail. I didn't kill Hanes."

"You're lying."

Scatlin ignored the accusation. "You're in a worse jam than ever. I'll be missed now and my friends will figure pretty close to what has happened." He grinned crookedly. "Being law-abiding citizens, they'll go right to the sheriff, and the posse will be scouring the country again. Something else—Tag will figure the same way and he won't like it a bit. You're going to be hunted and gunned down two ways."

"Do you figure you're that important?" Ken asked.

"I've done enough for Tag so he'll take care of me."

"Like killing Lou Hanes," Ken threw at him. "You're the one who can tie in that killing to Tag Nixon and Brad Moran. They planned this whole frame, and they'd hang for it if the truth came out."

"Ballard, you're the man who'll hang for this one."

"Maybe, but you'll be killed for it too. As long as you can talk, you'll be a threat to them. A careless drunken word from you and—" Ken made a cutting motion across his throat. "They'll not risk that."

A sudden doubt flared in Scatlin's pinched eyes and Ken could almost see his brain turning over the idea. Then the renegade sneered and sipped at his coffee again.

The coffee finished, Ken bound Scatlin securely. The man settled stubbornly against a wall, legs stretched out on the floor. "Now what you aim to do?"

Ken didn't answer. He searched the hills through the window and then went outside to check his horse. He had no real answer to Scatlin's question. How could he force the man to talk? Gun threat would mean nothing, for Scatlin knew Ken dared not kill him. Torture it out of him, using some of the methods Ken heard that the Apaches used in New Mexico? He shook his head, unable to bring himself to that except as a last resort. How, then?

He went back inside the shack. Scatlin didn't bother to look up. Ken dropped on the bunk, baffled but trying to hide it. Then he caught a look from the renegade, secretive, probing, uncertain and fearful. Ken pretended unconcern, stretching out and putting his arms under his head. Let the renegade's own nerves unravel—with a little help now and then from Ken.

He said in a matter-of-fact tone, "By the way, don't pin too much hope on being found by your friends."

After a moment Scatlin asked, "Why not?"

Ken opened his eyes as though aroused from a doze. "If they get too close, do you figure I'm going to hang onto you?"

He closed his eyes again and let the long minutes drag. Scatlin shifted restlessly, but Ken didn't move or open his eyes. He listened, though, and finally heard a soft movement over by the wall. Waiting a while longer, he heard more of the rustlings. He spoke without opening his eyes.

"You won't make the door."

The rustlings broke off and a tense silence filled the room. Ken could feel the gunhawk's hate-filled glare, but he didn't bother to move. His apparent assurance rubbed the man's guilty nerves.

After a time, Ken swung out of the bunk. Scatlin now sat well out from the wall and still some distance from the door. Ken smiled pleasantly at him and checked his food supply, hiding his dismay at the small amount of bacon, the few dried beans and the remaining flour. He stirred up the fire, placed the skillet on it and fried the bacon, warmed the beans. The odor filled the room and Scatlin's lips tightened.

The meal cooked, Ken took his plate to the bunk and started eating. Scatlin exploded, "What do you expect me to do?"

Ken shrugged. "Talk, that's all."

He continued eating. Scatlin glared, then cursed and worked his body around so that he could no longer watch the dwindling food on Ken's plate. Ken finished the scant meal, lingering over it. He reheated the coffee and stood in the open door-way, drinking it. He heard the renegade's irritable squirmings behind him, but continued watching the distant hills.

Unseen by his captive, Ken's eyes grew hard and grim as he looked out. This had become a three-way race, he thought, between the hunters, starvation, and Scatlin's confession. But he cleared the worry from his face before he turned.

"Ballard?" Scatlin said tentatively.

Ken stopped. "Going to talk about Lou Hanes?"

"No, damn it! I—"

"Then you're wasting your breath. But maybe you can be made to change your mind."

He stoked up the fire in the stove, lifted one of the rusted lids and placed a rusty poker in the flames. Scatlin stared, then searched Ken's face. Ken dropped on the bunk, watched the stove unconcernedly. Once, when the fire had burned to red hot embers, he arose, pushed the poker deeper and then sat down again.

Scatlin moistened his lips. "Ballard, what's that for?"

"You, maybe. I just thought of it."

"You're running a bluff."

"No, you are. Talk'll save us both a lot of time."

"Go to hell."

"Eventually . . . but you'll have a taste of it first."

The embers glowed as the minutes ticked by. Ken again examined the poker, lifting its dully glowing red tip so Scatlin could see it. He replaced it and, turning, saw the gunhawk's fear-shot eyes. Ken walked by him to the open door again and leaned on the jamb, looking out.

"Ballard?"

Ken didn't bother even to turn his head. "Yes?"

"Maybe we can make a deal."

"Sure. Tell me about Hanes."

"Damn you, I can't! I won't. There's nothing to tell."

"Well, that's one bit of truth. You can't tell—you're afraid of Nixon. Friend, what's the difference between a bullet and a hangrope?" Ken turned. "Now I'll make a deal. Talk, and I'll see you get a fair trial and some sort of consideration for putting the real blame where it belongs—on Nixon and Moran."

"What kind of a bargain's that?"

Ken nodded toward the stove and the ancient poker still in the embers. "Better than something like this."

Scatlin grunted derisively but didn't quite bring it off. Ken walked to the stove and considered the poker. "Of course, there are other ways. Ever see a man after his foot was caught in a stirrup and he was dragged by a horse? Then—Apaches down my way stake a man out and let the ants feed on him—or prop up his eyelids and make him watch the sun. There are lots of ways."

He moved to Scatlin, the poker in his hand. The man's mouth flew open and he hastily pulled in his feet, threw himself back toward the wall. Ken balanced the poker in his hand for a moment and then turned back to the stove. He placed the poker beside it and saw Scatlin tentatively straighten.

"Can't decide which way will make you open your mouth the fastest. It'll take some thinking."

He walked out of the shack and seated himself on the broken stoop. For a time there was silence within the shack and then he heard a faint rustling, then silence again. He looked around. Scatlin sat with his back against the wall, hands lashed behind him, feet tied. His head was thrown back, his eyes closed. The long thin body in the dirty underwear looked ridiculous. A muscle jumped in Ken's cheek. As ridiculous as a forked rattler, he thought. The fangs are still there.

Twilight came and Ken again fixed a scanty

meal. He shared this with Scatlin, gave him a bit of coffee and then made sure his bonds were secure. He rolled into his bunk and placed his gun to hand under his pillow, then watched the shadows deepen through the window and the partially open doorway.

"How about a blanket?" Scatlin abruptly asked. "Nights get cold."

Ken answered tightly, "The cold will keep you awake and thinking . . . about what's coming tomorrow. My patience can hold on just about that long."

Scatlin cursed. Ken swung out of the bunk and calmly gagged him. The man sputtered and mumbled, but Ken paid no attention as he returned to his bunk.

He awoke several times during the night. His sleep was light and troubled and the least sound snapped his eyes open. A slight shifting rustle when his prisoner relieved frigid, cramped muscles . . . the far-off mournful wail of a coyote . . . the shivering cry of a hunting owl. Most of the time he lay looking up at the darkness that hid the low ceiling. Food about gone, hunted, no way short of brutal torture to clear himself, Ken felt trapped. His slim hope lay in Scatlin's fears. The man would have them, since he could only think Ken would have the same cruel, killing instincts as himself.

Ken felt relieved when the dusty window

began to admit a faint light. It strengthened so that details of the room became clear. Scatlin lay on his side, legs drawn up, pressed against the wall, his eyes closed and his face slack in a tortured sleep. Ken checked any thoughts of sympathy for him and swung out of his bunk. As he watched, Scatlin stirred and opened his eyes.

Ken built a fire in the stove, disregarding the renegade's searching, fearful gaze that followed him as he moved about. He went outside and around the shack to check his horse and draw water from the old well. He looked around at the hills, golden bright now with the first rays of sun, then glanced up at the shack roof, the canted stove pipe that served as a chimney. A thin plume of blue smoke lifted straight into the air. Ken frowned. That would be a dead giveaway to searchers. As soon as coffee was brewed he'd kill the fire. For now, the need for the hot, warming liquid was worth the slight gamble.

An hour later, he knew that he'd have to carry out his bluff of violence, right up to the moment of torture itself. Scatlin was frightened, but not enough to talk. However, he was on the edge. Ken untied his ankles, jerked him to his feet. The man stumbled, caught himself by falling against the wall. He straightened and Ken propelled him toward the door.

Outside, Scatlin blinked against the bright sunlight and hopped painfully as his socked feet stepped on small rocks. He jerked away from Ken's grip, wheeled half around.

"What you aim to do?"

"You won't talk. I'll have to make you."

He propelled Scatlin around the corner of the shack and pushed him against the structure. "I reckon you won't get far in bare feet."

Ken left him, picked up his saddle and went to his horse. Bridled and ready, Ken swung into saddle, shook open his rope. Scatlin pressed against the wall and Ken grimly rode up to him. The renegade moved to avoid the skittering hoofs of the horse and Ken dropped the loop over him, tightened it.

He slowly moved the horse out from the wall and Scatlin hopped painfully at the end of the rope. Ken reined in and looked down, trying to hide his own uncertainty that this bluff would work.

"Your last chance. Who killed Lou Hanes?"

The renegade's eyes cut back and forth as though seeking escape. He clamped his jaws tightly and then shuddered. "You win, Ballard. I won't be dragged."

From the ridge of the steep hill above, a gun boomed and the slug cut between Ken and Scatlin, gouting dirt. Ken half turned, hand dropping to his gun.

"Just hold tight," a voice warned. "You ain't got a chance."

Further along, bushes swayed and Ken saw a man emerge, gun leveled. Scatlin's frightened eyes lighted. "Crane!"

Directly above Ken, a second man emerged and Scatlin's head swung around, his smile widening. "You found me! How'd you figure where to look?"

Crane worked his way down the steep slope while the second man kept his gun on Ken. Reaching level ground, Crane called up. "Join the party, Tomlin. Now ain't our friend a pretty sight?"

Ken remained frozen in the saddle as Crane's gun muzzle lined on him. Scatlin said impatiently, "Cut me loose. I sure got a debt to pay off."

Tomlin skidded down the slope and straightened. He moved forward, a grin breaking his stubbled face. His Colt swung loosely in the hand at his side. Scatlin twisted about.

"Cut me loose. Give me a gun!"

Crane watched Ken closely, then spoke to his partner. "Ain't it lucky we remembered this old hideout? Tag will be glad to hear the news."

"Tag?" Scatlin demanded eagerly.

"He's right in Sioux Springs to handle things. He got real worried about you, Hank. Wanted us to find you before the posse did. We knew Ballard must've run off with you."

"You've found me. Just unhitch me and give me a gun, and we'll take care of Ballard like we planned."

Neither of the renegades made a move. They exchanged looks and finally Crane said, "Hank, Tag's changed his plans a little."

"Tell me later."

"Well, seems he figures he don't want to run a risk like this again. So—"

His gun swung off Ken and lined on Scatlin. The Colt roared lancing flame, bucking back in Crane's thick fist. Scatlin catapulted back and down, his mouth still open to voice a startled protest.

XVI

Ken was hardly aware of what had happened. He had held his hands at shoulder height, eyes cutting to Tomlin, on his left. The renegade had not lifted his gun. Ken realized only that Crane's threatening Colt had swung away from him. In that split second before the gun roared, Ken's hand slashed to his Colt and he twisted about in the saddle.

Tomlin jerked around, gun lifting, twisting to bring it into line. Ken's Colt cleared the holster, snapped up and roared. Tomlin spun half around as Ken dropped from the saddle on the far side of the horse from Crane.

Crane whipped about, gun lifting to an empty saddle. It took him a split second to register that Ken had dropped to the ground. It was enough for Ken who, at a crouch, fired under the horse. The animal reared, and Ken dodged the churning hoofs. He dropped flat as the animal skittered to one side. His gun lined, but he checked the tightening of his finger on the trigger. Crane lay sprawled face down, his thick fingers futilely clawing into the ground. Even as Ken looked, his hand stopped moving and lay inert and lifeless.

Ken threw a look at Tomlin, who lay face up, one hand clutching at his red-stained shirt front, the other arm flung loosely to one side. Ken came swiftly to his feet, his attention centered on the bound figure in the long underwear. He felt a clutch of fear as he holstered his Colt and jumped to Scatlin's side.

The whole right side of the underwear had stained an ugly red and it slowly spread as Ken reached him. The man's eyes were closed. He still breathed, but Ken feared he would die and Lou Hanes' murder would thus be forever laid to his account.

Frantically tugging at the knots, Ken loosened the rope. He ripped open the underwear, buttons flying, and looked at the hole high up in the right side of the chest from which blood bubbled. Then he ripped out his handkerchief and started grimly to work.

He heard a slight stir and jerked around. Tomlin moved his head from side to side, his eyes still closed and his chest heaving. Ken turned again to Scatlin, alternately praying and cursing as he worked to stem the flow of blood.

Finally he succeeded, but he paused only for a breath of temporary relief. That wound looked deadly, and the man could still be bleeding internally. Ken had to get him to the nearest ranch, Sioux Springs, the sheriff's posse—anywhere that someone could bear witness to what the man might say if he recovered consciousness.

Just then Scatlin's eyelids fluttered and opened.

He stared up at Ken glassily; then reason flicked deep within his eyes. Ken cautioned, "Lay still for a while."

"He shot me," Scatlin said in soft wonder. "My own partner shot me!" His face contorted. "Tag told him to shut me up! To kill me, after all I did for him!"

"Take it easy," Ken cautioned.

Scatlin searched Ken's face for a moment. "I'm hit bad?"

"Real bad. I'll try to get you to a doctor."

"Do that. I want to live to see Tag and those two double-crossers hang."

"Crane and Tomlin are dead, or dying," Ken said.

"Then Tag Nixon—and Brad Moran. You're right, I shot Lou Hanes . . . on their orders. I made the signs lead to you, and any of us were to shoot you on sight, just to make sure. But it was—"

"Just keep your strength!" Ken said tightly. "Tell the right person. You got to hang on."

"I will. You can . . ."

His voice faded off and his eyes closed. Ken felt a clutch of fear until he saw the thin chest move and a check of the crude bandage showed no more bleeding. He stood up, moved to Crane. Ken's bullet had torn up through throat and mouth. Ken moved to Tomlin and knew nothing could be done for him. Life had fled, probably in the last minute or two. Ken went to get the gunmen's saddled horses. When he returned, a swift check showed Scatlin still lived. Ken pulled the two bodies into the shack where they could not be spotted by some nosy passerby. Then he broke up the bunk and, with adroit use of cut lengths of lariat, made a stretcher that could be swung between the two horses. Then he returned to Scatlin, looked fearfully at the pale, slack face and prayed the inevitable jars and jerks of moving him would not start the bleeding again.

Scatlin was placed at last, blanket thrown over him. Ken swung into his own saddle, holding the lead reins of the two horses, who nervously tossed their heads at this unusual burden. Ken moved out, across the meadow and into the maze of the hills. Now and then he turned to look at the wounded man. It would be a race with death, he knew—a death that could forever seal the truth behind motionless lips.

He headed directly for the town, not daring to waste time to search the hills for a ranch. The slow miles passed. Once he stopped and checked Scatlin. It seemed to him that the wound still leaked slowly, and Scatlin did not open his eyes as he worked. A cold fear clutching his heart, Ken remounted and desperately counted the remaining miles.

Time was running out, he knew, with each pump of Scatlin's laboring heart, with each drop of blood that seeped through the wound. Yet Ken dared not hurry; the constant jarring of trot or gallop would hasten the doom that Scatlin's condition promised.

Then, far off, he saw the first houses. Guns and hate waited him there, he knew, but he had to risk them. He looked back at Scatlin who, seemingly, had not moved. The buildings grew larger and then Ken saw the long run of the main street. His hand touched his holstered Colt, dropped away.

He passed the first houses. Ahead, men stopped on the sidewalks and stared at him in open-mouthed amazement. Someone shouted, and he saw a man run to the sheriff's office. Curious heads popped out of the barbershop and the stores, and men erupted from the saloons. Ken raised his hands high above his head as, to his surprise, he saw the sheriff burst out of his office, stare and then come striding to meet him.

An angry yell—"There's the killer! Hang him!"

The sheriff roared, "I'll shoot the first man who touches his gun!"

The lawman's Colt glinted in his hand as he leveled it on Ken and came striding up. "Ballard, you're under arrest."

Ken said desperately, "Get a doctor. This man's dying, but he has to talk before he cashes in."

The sheriff called an order and someone rushed away. Down the street Ken glimpsed men emerging from the stage station; then his heart leaped as he saw a slender figure in a gray dress step out the door of the station office. Ken's eyes returned to the lawman.

"Sheriff, I'm going to drop my gun." He lowered his hand slowly at the grim nod, carefully pulled his Colt from the holster and let it strike the dust of the street. He said, "I thought you'd be out hunting for me."

"We scoured the Treachery."

"I mean because I kidnaped him." His nod indicated Scatlin.

"This is the first I knew of it."

Ken understood then that Crane and Tomlin had not informed anyone. Tag Nixon, he thought grimly, had instantly seen a way to silence two threats—Scatlin and himself. Just then a harried man with a small bag pushed his way through the crowd and looked at Scatlin, still blanket-covered on the makeshift litter.

His voice came crisply. "Get him out from between those horses so I can look at him."

Ken started to move but the sheriff's gun checked him. Others jumped to obey the doctor's orders. Ken's eyes lifted and he saw Alice Hanes and Frank Sparks hurrying up. Sparks stopped short when he saw Ken; his handsome face twisted and his hand streaked for his gun.

Alice grabbed his wrist. "Frank! No!"

The sheriff looked over his shoulder and then turned, his Colt lined on Sparks. "That's right,

Frank—no. Leave your gun in the holster. This man's my prisoner."

The litter had been gently lowered and moved out from between the horses. The doctor threw back the blanket and examined the wound. Now he looked up, his lips set.

"He's about gone. Bleeding inside."

Ken asked desperately, "Can't he be brought around, Doc? He's got to talk!"

"Best to leave him alone to die in peace."

"If that happens, Doc, I hang for killing Lou Hanes."

The doctor's thin brows drew sharply down. Turning back to Scatlin, he opened his bag and took out bottles. He pressed something to Scatlin's nose, repeated it. A silence settled on the crowd; all of them watched in grim fascination.

Ken said, "Sheriff, I want you and me to talk to Scatlin if . . ."

The lawman nodded and Ken swung out of saddle. He and the sheriff bent over the dying renegade as the doctor worked. Scatlin's lips moved slightly and a whispered moan escaped.

Ken leaned forward as the doctor glanced up. "He just might come around for a few minutes."

Scatlin's eyelids fluttered, opened. His eyes looked glazed and unfocused. Then for a moment they cleared and recognized Ken, moved on to the sheriff.

Ken said, "You haven't got a chance to live—

just minutes. Crane killed you to shut you up. This is the sheriff, Scatlin. Tell him the truth. Tell him who shot Lou Hanes, and why."

Scatlin looked blank for a second and then his eyes blazed with fury. He tried to speak, failed, gathered strength and tried again. The words came faintly but the sheriff and the doctor, bending to the pallid lips, heard clearly enough.

The story came with agonizing slowness. Scatlin, Crane and Tomlin had trailed Lou Hanes from the moment he came to the station that fateful morning, waiting the time when they could kill without being seen. When he left town, they had made a fast, wide circle and waylaid him. Scatlin had fired the shot.

His eyes turned to Ken and his voice faltered, then gained strength again. "Night before . . . his neckerchief . . . stole from hotel . . . planted . . . we said we saw him . . . lie . . . joined posse . . . to shoot him down before he was caught." The man's chest heaved but he caught his voice again. ". . . or kill him on way to . . . jail. . . ."

The eyes began to glaze. Ken's hand grabbed the thin shoulder. "Scatlin, who ordered you to kill Hanes?"

Silence for seconds that seemed an eternity. Then the faint whisper. "Tag . . . it was . . . he told us . . . Tag. . . ."

A rattle choked off the words and the chest and throat fought for breath that would not come.

The thin body collapsed and Scatlin was gone. The doctor shrugged and stood up as Ken and the sheriff straightened. A strange sigh swept the close-pressing crowd. Ken realized that Frank Sparks and Alice had worked their way to the side of the litter.

He met the girl's pain-filled eyes, which softened as she looked at him. His brief smile sent her momentary thanks for the time she had given him to have a chance of clearing himself. Sparks looked down at the thin body; then his dark eyes lifted to Ken's, probing and searching, as though he sought some sign of trickery. His tight face seemed to mask an inner disappointment.

The sheriff broke the silence. "I reckon that clears you of the Hanes killing, Ballard. Lucky we didn't catch you, up on the Treacheries."

"You came close," Ken said. "I figured what had happened and why, so I slipped back here to find him."

He briefly told of kidnaping Scatlin, of the swift and deadly battle with the two gunslingers after Crane had deliberately carried out his order to execute Scatlin. Suddenly Ken jerked erect.

"Tag Nixon! He was in town. He's the one who ordered the killings."

"Nixon!" Sparks exclaimed.

The sheriff whipped around and shoved a path through the crowd. Ken bent to scoop up his Colt and then followed after him as the lawman strode to the hotel. Sparks cursed under his breath and lunged forward, quickly overhauling Ken and then the lawman. As he and the sheriff mounted the steps, Ken glanced down the street toward the livery stable. He glimpsed a big, heavy figure dart through the wide doors.

"Sheriff!" Ken yelled. "Nixon's running! The stable!"

They whipped about as Ken raced toward the distant building. He heard their boots thudding behind him, and drew his gun. Nixon had to be stopped, had to be captured, so the link between Scatlin, Nixon and Moran could be made clear.

The big gunhawk must have kept his horse saddled, or else he had grabbed the first mount ready to ride. Ken, Sparks and the lawman were still racing toward the stable when a rider burst out the doors. Ken caught the glint of metal and threw himself to one side as Nixon slammed a shot at him.

The spurs raked cruelly and the horse bolted down the street. Ken fired, wanting to bring down the horse rather than chance killing Nixon. He heard another gun thunder just beside him, and Sparks' furious yell. Nixon swayed, grabbed the saddlehorn.

A moment later he fell and the horse bolted away down the street and out of town. Ken yelled in triumph and ran forward. Nixon came to his feet, dropped, struggled to get up again.

Beside Ken, Sparks cursed and leveled his Colt. Ken saw the killing fury in Sparks' drawn face and he swung around, hand straining to knock up the Colt. But before he could touch it, the weapon thundered and bucked. The slug caught Nixon in the chest, drove him back and down into the dust.

Ken forgot Sparks. He rushed to the fallen man, then stopped short. Sparks' bullet had smashed the life out of the heavy body. The superintendent came up, lips pulled back against his teeth. Just behind him raced the sheriff.

Sparks leveled his gun at the dead man, and then Ken's fury broke. He whirled about and his fist pistoned up and cracked off Sparks' jaw. It was a glancing blow but the man, caught off balance, went down.

Ken glared down at the fallen man, only dimly hearing the sheriff's surprised yell. "You fool! You damn fool!"

Sparks' blank face suffused with dark fury. He still held his gun and he swung it up, black muzzle lining.

XVII

The sheriff's blunt boot toe connected with the gun, sending it spinning from Sparks' hand. The man moved swiftly into a fighting crouch and tried to launch himself beyond the sheriff at Ken. The lawman grabbed him, sent him sprawling. Sparks again came to his feet but abruptly rocked back on his heels when he found himself looking down the black muzzle of the sheriff's gun.

"Hold it, Frank! So help me, I'll break your leg with a slug if you so much as take a step! There's been too much fighting, shooting and killing around here."

Their glaring eyes locked. Frank choked, "He'll pay for that. No one knocks me down and gets away with it."

Ken said, "I lost my head. He shot to kill Nixon."

"Why shouldn't I? He had Lou shot. He was a murdering sidewinder!"

Ken spoke to the sheriff. "Maybe we'd better talk this over where too many people won't hear."

"Who are you to say where we'll talk?" Sparks blazed.

The lawman turned on him. "Frank, if you don't get your brains back in your head, I might beat 'em back in for you. You've been breathing fire and blood and flying off the handle since this whole thing started. Now we calm down and try to make some sense out of this mess, do you understand?"

Sparks' lips pressed tightly and he looked ready to explode. Finally he walked to where his gun lay, scooped it up and dropped it in the holster. He glanced at Nixon's heavy body and a pleased light came in his eyes as he strode back toward the hotel and the sheriff's office.

Alice Hanes had moved out of the crowd to meet them. Her worried glance moved from Ken to Sparks and back again. She had seen the angry flurry from a distance but, at the moment, she only nodded when the sheriff said shortly, "We'd like to use your office, Miss Alice."

A short while later, the four of them formed a strained group in the small office. The sheriff had ordered the disposal of the bodies in the street and had sent some deputies to bring in Crane and Tomlin for burial. Now he looked from Ken to Alice to Sparks, who sat at Lou's desk as though he had inherited it. Then the sheriff's grim, tired eyes turned to Ken again.

"I reckon there's a lot about this none of us understand. It looks like you're the only one who can clear it up."

Ken nodded. "And I won't show up very pretty, Sheriff. Miss Alice knows how Moran tried to use me. I've told her."

"When did you tell her?" Sparks demanded.

The girl's cool voice cut in. "He came back here while you were hunting him in the Treacheries—came to me out at the ranch. I nearly shot him, but—"

"Got scared!" Frank snapped. "Thought you saw someone! And you did—him! Why didn't you tell me?"

"You wouldn't have understood." She looked down at her hands. "Frankly, I don't know myself why I believed him—until today."

"Now look, Alice—"

"Frank!" the sheriff roared. "I want to hear Ballard's story, and I want to hear it now!"

The superintendent seethed but fell silent. Ken took a breath and then told the whole story, from his kidnaping out of the hobo jungle right up to bringing the dying Scatlin into town.

"We needed Tag Nixon alive and up on trial for murder," he concluded. "Face a man like that with a hangrope and he'd try to save his neck by telling the truth about Moran. But what can we do now? Scatlin's dead, so are Crane and Tomlin. Scatlin accused Nixon—and now Nixon's dead. There's suspicion aplenty against Moran but he can laugh at it. What can we do?"

The sheriff scratched his head and sighed. "You've got the right of it."

"You mean," Sparks demanded, "that Moran will get off free and easy and—"

"You made it that way," the sheriff growled,

"with your hot temper and fast gun. Ballard's right. We can't do a thing to Moran, or show any proof that a judge and jury would listen to."

Alice sighed, looking from one man to the other. "What will he do?"

The lawman shook his head. "Anything he wants, I guess. If he comes to Sioux Springs, he can laugh at all of us."

"And he'll come," Ken said flatly.

"He won't stay long," Sparks growled.

The sheriff stood up. "So long as Moran keeps within the law, he can stay as long as he pleases. Frank, remember that. Keep your head, for once, and handle this right. If you try gunplay, I just might have you in jail waiting for trial."

Sparks fumed but said nothing. The lawman walked to the door. "Nothing more I can do here. Ballard, all of us can thank you for turning up Lou's killer—and for ridding the county of a few snakes. I guess I owe you an apology for chasing you all over the Treacheries."

"You did what you had to, Sheriff. No hard feelings—then or now."

The lawman nodded, spoke a word to Alice, gave Sparks a long and warning look and left. The two men and the girl were silent, each deep in his own thoughts, turning over the grim possibilities.

At last Alice said slowly, "Maybe Moran won't come."

"Why figure that?" Ken asked.

She looked hopefully at him. "Well, look what he's lost—three gunslingers, not counting his ramrod Nixon. It's gained him nothing."

Sparks' hand slapped down on the desk. "He won't dare show."

"What do you think, Ken?" Alice asked.

She flushed, realizing she had instinctively used the familiar first name. Ken caught Sparks' probing look and tried to pass off the slip as though he hadn't noticed.

"He's lost men, that's true," he said slowly. "But nothing else. He wants to break in up here and he's used murder to do it. Your father's gone; Moran will figure people won't believe a woman can handle this business."

"But I've been Father's partner! Everyone knows that."

"Sure—but here in the office. Merchants and shippers knew your father, or Sparks here. They were the ones who rode the routes and managed the schedules, met the shippers."

"Then you think . . ."

"Moran will go to every ranch, town, and merchant. He'll hint that a petticoat can't handle a freight line, and the business will go to pot. He'll cut rates, too, and that'll help him pick up business. Maybe he'll bring in more trouble-makers. I'm sure Nixon and the other three aren't the only gunslingers on his payroll."

"They'll get lead for lead," Sparks snapped.

"It's right they should, but that won't come at first."

"What will?" Alice asked.

"Moran himself, everywhere along the line. He'll say Hanes Freight Lines is in trouble, and he'll get people to listen—unless . . ."

He frowned, thinking. Alice leaned forward. "Unless?"

"Maybe we—you—should beat him to it. Send someone out right now so they'll know nothing's changed. Do it before Moran can get in his licks. The shippers liked and trusted Lou and they'll want to stick if they're sure of service."

Alice fired to the thought, smoke-violet eyes alight. "We'll do it! I'll start first thing in the morning."

Ken made an embarrassed gesture. "Better not you, Miss Alice." Her face fell, puzzled, and he hurried on. "Men don't like doing business direct with a woman. They might someday, but not now. Better send a man to do the talking."

"But they'll know that I own the line!"

"They won't see you and deal with you, except now and then. It'll take a man for this job. Sparks, here, would be the one."

Sparks looked surprised, but his dark face lighted. He nodded. "They know me."

Alice considered, soft lips pursed. She looked

at Sparks, at Ken, back at Sparks again, then said slowly, "I don't know."

"I've been up and down every route," Sparks said vehemently. "I've handled complaints and—"

"I know, Frank. But sometimes you've angered our customers. Father had to smooth things over." She made a small gesture as he stared at her, surprised and angered. "You can handle the men and the routine at the stations, Frank. I need you there."

"But who—"

Her eyes cut to Ken. "I think Mr. Ballard."

"Him! But he's not even working for us!"

"He is. That is, if he will, after all that's happened." She turned directly to Ken. "Will you?"

She leaned toward him and the light caressed the smooth delicate contours of her face, highlighted the corners of her mouth and made a halo of her hair. Ken spoke instantly, without thought, out of an overwhelming desire to help her in the struggle that was bound to come.

"Of course I'll work for you—but I'm not sure about this."

"I am," she interrupted flatly. "About myself, I agree. I also know where Frank is needed most. You're new, but you're a man, and I think people will like you right away. Seeing customers is your job."

Ken dropped back in his chair. He saw Sparks'

dark and angry face and sensed the man was close to explosion. He stood up. "I'll think it over. You do, too. By tomorrow morning we should all know what's best."

He saw the protest forming on Alice's lips, but he hurried through the swing gate and out of the office.

When he had left, Sparks jerked to his feet. He choked back angry words, finally spoke in a falsely calm voice. "I reckon you know what you're doing?"

"I think so, Frank."

"But *him!*" Frank snarled. "Him!"

"We owe him the job."

"A Moran spy! You heard him say what he was supposed to do—and he did it!"

Her voice became edged, but Frank didn't notice. "I also heard why he did it—at gunpoint, really. I also know he tried to pull out. More than that, I know he has warned us about Moran and is willing to fight on our side."

"Oh, you know!" Frank's voice held acid sarcasm. "It's just his word, and who's to prove it but him? But that's enough for you, ain't it? I've seen the way you look at him and—"

"Frank! That's enough!"

His lips snapped shut but his mouth formed an ugly line. Then he shrugged and spoke more calmly. "I reckon it is, Alice. I say too much and sometimes I don't say what I mean. I don't want anything to happen to you—like Ken Ballard."

"What's wrong with him?"

"Maybe nothing—maybe everything. I don't like him; I admit it. I don't trust him. Easy as not, he could have tricked Scatlin into confessing to a murder he didn't do."

"What!"

"The man was wounded and dying, half out of his head. He figured he'd been doublecrossed, and it wouldn't take much for Ballard to persuade him to lie to hang Moran or Nixon."

"But why?" She came to her feet, her small chin jutted out. "Frank, I think you'd better go home and think over what you've said. It doesn't make sense except to a man who's crazy with . . ."

Her voice trailed off. Frank nodded, finished for her. "Jealousy? Yes, I'll admit that, too. Forget what I said, except for one thing. Don't trust Ballard. I don't."

He turned to the door. "I'll be out in the warehouse. Lots to be done." He hesitated. "About tomorrow—who goes, him or me?"

She didn't answer, but sat down again and opened a big ledger. Frank waited, saw the stubborn set of her shoulders. He turned with an angry jerk of the body and stalked out of the office.

When Ken came into the office the next day, Sparks was not in sight. Alice looked up from her desk, her bright, warm smile making him welcome. Ken smiled in return and then looked back out in the yard toward the warehouse and stables. He could not see Sparks.

Alice's voice brought him around. "Ready for work?"

"Sure—whatever it is."

"Seeing our shippers. I've decided you were right, and that you're the man."

Ken moved into the office, slowly moving his hatbrim around in his fingers. He glanced toward the yard again. "Are you sure this is right, ma'am?"

"Can't we be less formal?" she asked.

"Sure, Miss Alice."

"Well, that's better." She sobered. "Yes, I think you're the right person. As I said, Frank has antagonized people. And that is something we can very much do without right now."

"This could antagonize him," Ken suggested.

"Let's understand one another, Ken. Frank has no reason to be angry, really. I'm free to pick and choose, and to run this business as I think best. I chose you for this job, Frank for another."

He studied her. She looked away, but he could read the steadfast determination in her expression. He broke the silence. "Okay, Miss Alice. I'll do the job."

Strain left her and her face lifted, bright and eager. "Where will you start?"

"Well, best place is right where the hauling starts—Pass City. Wholesalers down there ship to merchants up here, and they're the ones Moran will first try to get away from you. Dry up Pass City and the rest of the line will die."

She nodded, then suddenly looked worried. "But that's putting you right in Moran's hands!"

Ken smiled tightly. "He won't bother with me—for a while. After what happened up here, he'll not take too many risks."

"When will you go?"

"First thing in the morning. Can I have a list of our shippers down there? And maybe a note to the station manager, so he'll know who I am?"

"This afternoon."

The next morning, Ken saddled his horse and rode out of Sioux Springs. Since he had gotten his lists and last-moment suggestions from Alice the afternoon before, he did not go to the freight station.

He rode at a steady pace that ate up the miles but did not tire the horse. The low, dark line of the Treachery Range, to the south, slowly grew larger and lifted into the sky. Nightfall found him in camp not far from the mouth of Treachery Pass.

He was up early in the morning and again in the saddle, after a light breakfast cooked over his campfire. He passed the place where Hal Smith had tried to capture him, and he smiled crookedly.

Strange, he thought, the twists and changes that could come in a life.

He now rode the pass itself, the road climbing steadily in a series of loops and curves. In this broken mountain country, rocks or trees blocked all but short sections of the road. Nearing the crest of the pass, Ken rode around one of the curves and jerked erect in the saddle.

A rider sat his horse at the edge of the road, one leg hooked over the saddlehorn. As Ken came in view, the man straightened, lifted the reins and came slowly forward. Ken reined in, narrowly watching Frank Sparks approach.

The superintendent came steadily on and halted a few feet away. His dark handsome face told nothing and he veiled all but a faint spark far back in his dark eyes. He nodded, said flatly, "I thought I'd meet you somewhere along this stretch."

Ken cuffed back his hatbrim. "Something wrong?"

"Not so far as you're concerned—that's plain."

"Meaning what?"

"Meaning you've worked yourself into a good job and I figure you plan to work yourself in pretty strong with Alice."

Ken folded his hands over the saddlehorn. "I'm thankful for the job. But I'm working at nothing else."

"I could call you a liar."

"You could, but don't. Sparks, you and I have been over this before. You're as wrong now as you were then."

Sparks lost some of his impassive mask. His lips curled. "I believe you about as much. Still, I reckon we can come to some sort of understanding, seeing we're working together—right now."

Ken nodded. "Now that's sense. I want no kind of trouble."

"You won't get it, so long as you do your job— and nothing else. I have plans for Alice and me and I am not going to let anyone upset them."

"Does she know about these plans?"

Sparks held back his temper. "She will, and she has some idea of them already. So I've staked out the claim until I can make it legal. As long as you keep your distance, maybe we can get along."

Ken studied the man and suddenly laughed. Frank's features broke into a grimace of fury as Ken said, "Sparks, I sure wish I had your confidence. Here you're dabbing a loop on a girl who doesn't even know it yet. Have you figured she might have other ideas?"

"Like you? A wandering saddlebum!"

Ken choked back his chuckles. "No, not like me. But that still don't make you the top man in her mind. And something tells me you never will be."

Sparks' hand dropped to his holster, but Ken's

hand blurred and his Colt lined on the super-intendent. Sparks stared at the gun, then slowly loosened his grip around his own, which was still within leather.

Ken slowly tilted up the muzzle, eying Sparks over it. Then he dropped the Colt back into the holster. "I didn't want to do that, Sparks. I don't want to have to do it again. Get this straight. Lou Hanes and Alice helped me start a new life and I began to believe in people like them again. I want to repay their confidence in me. Lou's dead, but Alice is still around. I'll work for her as long as she needs me. I hope I can work with you."

He lifted the reins. "Of course, I don't have the full say. A lot of it's up to you. I'll see you when I get back from Pass City."

He touched his hatbrim, neck reined the horse and rode on, rounding the far turn without once looking back. After he had disappeared, Sparks rubbed his hand along his holster, his fingers caressing the handle of the heavy Colt. Then he jerked his hand away and muttered under his breath.

"A sneak and a liar! Work with him? And watch him walk off with her? I'd see them both in hell first!"

He neck reined his horse and cruelly raked the spurs. The animal reared, snorted and bolted away, north toward Sioux Springs.

XVIII

Two weeks later Ken rode back into Sioux Springs. As he passed one of the saloons he saw three men standing at the rail of the porch. They wore holstered guns low on their right legs, and a single glance told him the kind of men they were. His eyes grew bleak. Word of this had brought him north, even though he should have remained in Pass City.

He angled toward the freight station, but as he started by the sheriff's office the lawman appeared in the doorway and signaled him over. Ken turned in and the sheriff came to the edge of the porch. He looked back toward the saloon.

"Know any of those vultures over there, Ballard?"

"Not personal. Gunhawk breed, though."

"Plain to see," the lawman grunted. "Them and a round dozen more come swooping in maybe ten days or more ago. Been trouble up this way since then. One thing fits with the other."

"Trouble?"

"Stores robbed here and there. A couple of fires. Hardware man up in Red Cloud waylaid by five men and beaten near to death."

"Any of these?"

"They were masked, all five. Might've been every one—or none—of 'em."

Ken had looked back over his shoulder. Now he turned to face the sheriff again. "Can't you run 'em out?"

"They got money—so they're not vagrants, even if they don't seem to work. There's not a dodger on them from anywhere. They don't disturb the peace, they don't start fights. They don't even spit in the street! So what can I do? I hoped maybe you could tie 'em in with Nixon or Scatlin and that bunch."

"I wish I could."

The lawman grunted. "Too bad. I been running all over the county chasing down trouble that just plain vanishes by the time I get where it happened. It's tied in with Moran, but I can't prove it."

Ken straightened, lifted the reins. "I figured that would happen."

"Then figure what they'll do before they do it," the sheriff said shortly. "That's the only way I know how to catch 'em red handed, even with Brad Moran here."

"Moran! In town?"

"Staying big as life and smooth as silk at the hotel. Grins every time he sees me and I sure ache to have some reason to wipe the grin off his face. Well, thanks anyhow, Ballard."

He turned back into his office and Ken slowly rode on to the freight station. When he came into the yard he saw two wagons parked along the far

227

fence, a definite sign that business had fallen off. He frowned at the sight and then erased the frown when the office door burst open and Alice appeared.

"Ken! You're back!"

He smiled. "And glad to be. Let me off saddle and I'll be in to talk to you."

She nodded and he rode on, aware that she watched after him for a moment before she turned back into the office. He rode to the stable, dismounted and turned the horse over to a hostler. Then he turned to the warehouse, and mounted the steps to the loading dock.

The foreman, Hal Smith, came wandering up, hands shoved deep in his pockets. Ken saw three roustabouts playing cards on a packing crate, and the whole big, roofed area seemed to echo with emptiness.

He said grimly, "Looks like there's not enough work to kill us."

Hal indicated his bare work stand. "Half a dozen shipping memos, when there used to be twenty or thirty."

"Who's getting the business? Moran?"

"Some—what there is. What's happening in Pass City?"

"Nothing good. But I hope for better."

"Keep saying that! Miss Alice isn't saying much but I'll bet she's near broke. Won't cut down by laying anyone off. Says she doesn't want to do that and she's sure shipping will pick up. She whistles loud in the dark, I'll give her credit for that."

"It's like her."

Ken gave another glance at the nearly empty cavern and jumped down off the dock. He crossed to the office and entered. Alice was sitting at her desk by the window, but she wheeled around and stood up as Ken came in. He saw that the spindle of shipping charges was almost bare and the big ledger book was closed.

She opened the barrier gate for him. "A good trip, Ken?"

"Riding there and back, yes. In Pass City it could have been better."

She indicated a chair by her desk and sank into her own. He swept off his hat and sat down. Light from the window clearly showed the tiny worry lines about the girl's eyes, the unconsciously grim set of her soft lips.

He plunged into his report without preliminaries, knowing it was kinder to tell the bad news swiftly. "By the time I reached Pass City, Moran had already been at work. Even before I could get there he had spread word that your father was killed. Proves he knew what was going to happen."

He paused, respecting the small spasm of grief that crossed her face and clouded her eyes for a moment. "He had every big shipper down there certain that Hanes Freight Lines would fold come morning and be ready to sign up with him. Lucky for us they liked Lou and decided to wait and see. I persuaded most of them to stick with us."

"I know, Ken. But we're having trouble anyway."

"Chalk it up to Moran. He's spent money to break us. Railroad freight handlers send our shipments astray so our wagons can't pick them up. One freight car went clear to Arizona! Moran had bribed the conductor and engineer. No proof, of course. Just looked like a stupid mistake. But somehow all these things come to look like our fault when the shippers hear about them."

She sighed. "It's the same up here. We lost rolling stock, freight and horses in a station fire. A hostler knocked over a lantern. We haven't seen him since. Could have been an accident, but . . ."

"He could have been paid to do it?"

She nodded. "Yes. We've lost teamsters. Masked men caught one on the road, pulled him off the wagon, and used a blacksnake whip. He nearly died. Another found himself in a barroom fight up north—a saloon that had never had a bit of trouble before. Supposedly a drunken bunch of chuckline riders. But no one was hurt except our man. One teamster found his house afire and barely saved himself and his wife. They're beginning to be afraid to work for us."

"Nothing to tie these things to Moran?" Ken asked.

"Nothing at all. He's right here in town, bold as brass. He had the nerve to walk in here the first day he arrived in town. Pretended he'd just heard about Father and was so very, very sorry! Offered to buy me out, but you can imagine what I told him!"

Ken smiled tightly. She went on, "I told him we knew who had been behind Nixon and those other three. He was all hurt innocence! Oh, sure, Nixon had worked for him, but Mr. Moran had fired him when he found out the kind of man Nixon was. Strange, that was only a few days before Father was killed! Mr. Moran did not even know Scatlin and the others—or so he claimed! We've done him quite an injustice, Ken! And by the way, there's no record of you ever being on his payroll—anywhere. He can't imagine why you told those wild tales about him!"

Ken sighed, grimaced. "I told you he'd clear himself. The sheriff told me things are happening to our customers, too."

"Poor man! He's run ragged—everywhere."

"Moran must have his gundogs operating in small groups. Hit here, ride fast and hard, ride somewhere else and hit. Four-five bunches like that can scatter damage all over."

"That's what's happening."

Ken's fist doubled. "What are we doing about it?"

Her lip trembled on the edge of futile tears. "All we can. But we're hitting at shadows. What *can* we do, Ken?"

She turned to him in appeal. He saw the glisten of tears in the smoke-violet eyes and his heart wrenched. But he had no immediate answer, and that made him seethe inwardly. However, he kept an outward calm.

"There has to be some loose end of the rope somewhere that ties in to Moran. I'll try to find it. Keep Sparks troubleshooting and fighting. That'll keep Moran's attention while I look for sign."

She nodded and impulsively reached forward, placing slender fingers on his hand. The touch was warm and electric. "You have to find it, Ken! We can't last much longer."

His hand turned and engulfed hers. Their eyes held for a long moment and silently revealed each to the other. It was a moment of truth, and of shock. It had come so suddenly and surprisingly that neither was prepared to face it. Her eyes moved away first and she pulled back her hand. Ken was not sure, later, in what manner he left the office.

He carried his bedroll to the hotel, registered and went to a room at the rear of the building. His window gave a view of the three or four streets to the east, lined with squat small houses and, beyond, the open rolling range leading to distant hills. He gave it a glance, glad that he could not look at the station and see the girl seated alone in the office. He still felt the shaking experience of the few moments before, and right now he needed to find his balance.

He bathed and changed his dusty clothing, and had just finished when a knock on the door swung him around. He took a step toward it and then caution checked him. Swinging to the bed, he snapped the gunbelt about his waist. Then he pulled the door open.

Brad Moran looked up at him with a faint smile on his thin lips, brows cocked questioningly. The strangely shifting eyes held Ken for a moment, swung around the room and then back to Ken. "Do you think we can talk?"

Ken recovered. "That's the last thing I'd want to do. I'm surprised that you—"

"You should know better," Moran cut in. He strode by Ken and into the room, took the single chair and sat down.

Ken was on the verge of ordering him out, but then he slowly closed the door and stood before it. Moran still dressed like a lawyer or a drummer, he saw, and there was no sign of a gun about him. But Ken discounted that.

Moran said easily, "I underrated you, Ballard, and that's something I seldom do."

"Not exactly. I didn't see your trap until I fell into it."

"That was Nixon's idea, not mine."

Ken shifted his weight. "I'm not the sheriff. Legally, he has to believe you until he can prove different. I don't."

"Neither does the sheriff." Moran shrugged. "And what can either of you do?"

"You could stop a bullet."

"Anyone can, Ballard. Like four friends of mine, thanks to you. At first I was very bitter toward you; then I saw I should really admire you. Fast thinking and fast gun work—I didn't think you had either."

Ken said dryly, "Thanks. And now what?"

"I'd like to ask you that."

"Simple. I want to break up your game and see you hang for Lou Hanes' murder."

"Can't be done. Nothing ties me to the Hanes business. No one can prove I ordered it or was behind it. As for the other business, I'm moving in. The woman over there is already badly hurt. Before long she'll be lucky to be hauling firewood in those wagons of hers."

"That remains to be seen." Ken eyed the dapper and dangerous man. "But why are you bothering with me?"

"Let's say I have a new respect for you. Not fear, understand—respect. You think fast, and you're a realist."

"Meaning?"

Moran ticked off on his fingers. "Item one—the girl can't stand the losses. Item two—shippers don't like delays and straying shipments. Item three—they like cut rates and sure service. Item four—bad luck rides the Hanes wagons, and everybody's afraid of it. Item five and last—I intend to take over, easy or hard, and some of that depends on you."

"Think again! You used me once, but no more. I'll fight you to the last inch of hide."

"Fine for you, if you like it that way. But what about her? Going to let her lose everything she's got because you don't like me?" Moran saw he had scored a point. "Like I said, you think fast and you can see what's ahead. I don't intend to buy, hire or use you, Ballard. That's all over. But you could figure the girl could sell out for a decent figure now instead of going broke in a few weeks."

"Why buy her out if you're so sure?"

Moran stood up. "Saves time, saves trouble, and I don't like to see a woman hurt—even if I have to do it. Tell her she can talk to me anytime. Or don't tell her, if that's the way you feel. Either way, I'll know in a day or two."

He brushed by Ken and walked out, closing the door softly behind him.

Ken strode up and down the narrow room. He wanted no compromise with Moran and yet he had to admit the man was right. He could not pull Alice to bankruptcy because of his own hatred of the man. He cursed Moran under his breath. How cleverly he could use a man's own character, or lack of it, for his own ends! Ken snatched up his hat and strode from the room.

When he had told Alice the whole story, she dropped back in her chair. Her fingers absently traced over the ledger and her eyes became dark and distant. She said in a low voice, "He's right. I can't last much longer. These 'accidents' bleed us white."

Ken started to speak, then clamped his lips. The silence stretched on and on before she looked at him. "What do you think?"

"It's not my say; it's not my business."

"I know, but what do you say? What would you do?"

"Moran wants the business; nothing else matters to him. He'll get it by buying or destroying it. He'll drive you down in price if you try to sell, knowing he has the aces."

"That bothers you?"

"Some, but it's not the main reason. Selling to Moran means he's made murder pay off—your father's. I told him I'd fight him to the last breath. But that's me, not you."

"It's also me, Ken. I'd already made up my mind, but I wondered what you'd say." Again that impulsive grasping of his hand, the touch gone in a second. "So let's fight him."

He laughed and stood up. "I'll ride tomorrow—north."

He opened the door, but her voice checked him. "Ken, thank you. Very, very much. If we win . . ."

Her voice drifted off, but something in her eyes and the soft shape of her lips continued to speak a silent promise that held Ken rooted for a moment. Then he hurried out into the yard, not daring to believe.

XIX

Two weeks of futile searching and riding brought Ken full circle back to Pass City. He had forced himself to disregard news of breakdowns and trouble along the routes and in the scattered stations of the freight line, leaving that to Sparks. He had looked for something that would definitely and legally tie Moran to assault, theft, arson or intimidation.

There had been nothing. Hard-eyed, gunslung men had taken part, but everyone was a stranger who had disappeared soon after and later reappeared somewhere else. Moran himself remained in Sioux Springs or traveled openly to Pass City. Once he had walked into the Sioux Springs office and had offered Alice Hanes a price for the business. She had refused.

Now, back in Pass City, Ken felt he had wasted precious time. More shippers had dropped away, more wagons had broken down, more drivers had suddenly quit, with fear deep in their eyes but saying nothing. Ken knew that Moran was pulling the last frazzled end of the string through their hands but knew they could do nothing about it.

Confirmation came when the Pass City station manager talked discouragedly to Ken in his office. "Laid off some of the workers, Ballard, and told Miss Alice she'd just have to make do. No point in her paying out lost wages to men who can get jobs somewhere else."

"It's that bad?"

"Clean down. Take the War Bonnet Mining Company. Hanes had all their shipping—timber, hardware, and supplies; we even slipped the monthly payroll among the cartons and barrels. Last month Jeff Hayden acted funny, but we got the job. Now here it is time for payroll again and I can't get him to so much as talk to me."

Ken sighed. He knew War Bonnet was the last of their big customers. If they went over to Moran the remaining little shippers would scamper away, too. He summoned up a bit of courage from the depths of his despair. "Let me see what I can do."

"You know Hayden?"

"Never met him, but I will."

"I don't know, Ballard. Jeff and Hanes were close friends. Lou loaned him money ten years back when Hayden was in a tight bind. Saved him from going under, I hear. But now that Lou's gone . . ."

"Nothing like asking," Ken said flatly.

From the moment Ken shook hands with Hayden and sat down, he realized the man was on the defensive. Hayden covered it by making Ken welcome, and asking about Alice, but he could not help the little nervous play of his fingers in the wisp of an iron-gray beard that covered his cleft chin.

His distress became more apparent when Ken came directly to the point. "We've been expecting word from you this month about the payroll shipment."

"Ah . . . yes. Well, we haven't quite decided how we'll handle it this time."

"Something wrong with Hanes?" Ken asked sharply.

Hayden's eyes slid away to his desk and he slowly shook his head. "No, nothing wrong. But . . . well, that amount of money is always a lure, and it's been handled the same way now for several years."

"But this time?"

"Well . . . we've been thinking some of the wrong people might know the routine by now. So, to play safe, you understand, we might have one of our own men carry it. Perhaps I might do it myself."

Ken sat silent for a long moment and Hayden moved uncomfortably. Finally Ken said, "Who's going to haul your regular supplies and material? We've not had word on that, either."

Hayden answered cautiously, "We have to consider that, too."

Ken leaned forward. "I guess you've heard of trouble up around Sioux Springs?"

"Oh, a rumor or two. We discounted it; we're always hearing them."

Ken took a shot in the dark. "From Brad Moran?"

Hayden's startled, guilty look told the story. Ken nodded grimly. "Let's talk straight, Hayden. Moran hints that what happened up there could happen to your shipments and to your equipment and mines."

"I did talk to Mr. Moran. But I can't say that he threatened us."

"Not in so many words, but I figure it came through clear as a smoke signal. So you're jumping the way he wants you."

Hayden bristled, but without real anger. "Mr. Ballard, it's plain good business to be careful!"

"Was Lou Hanes?"

"Eh?"

"When he loaned you money some years back. You'd be bankrupt and working for wages now if Lou hadn't thrown 'good business' out the window and helped you."

Hayden flushed and Ken pressed on. "I've heard Lou Hanes was your best friend. Nothing could come between you."

"That's true—"

"But now he's been murdered." Ken stood up. "I've got no proof, but Moran was behind that. Anyhow, we know his men did it. Now he scares you into swinging his way. That's enough, ain't it? Lou's dead, so you owe nothing to him, his memory—or his daughter, who's trying to hold things together."

Hayden looked miserable. Ken walked to the door, turned. "I'll tell you something. She *will* hold it together—with or without you. But you can figure where you'll stand when word gets out Lou's best friend ran off and let his daughter go busted, for all he cares."

"You don't understand!" Hayden said in a muffled voice.

"Maybe I don't. I'll be over at the station a couple of days longer. Maybe you can help me understand by then. Good day, sir."

Hayden's full face was heavy and stricken when Ken opened the door and strode through the outer office to the street. Only after he was some distance away did he stop and look back at the office. Now he felt uncertainty, a nagging fear that he had further alienated Hayden. Yet he knew that a long argument would not have dispelled the man's fears of Moran. Only loyalty to a friend could do it, and even that was shaken. Ken mentally crossed his fingers when he thought of the next two days.

Late that afternoon, Frank Sparks rode into the station. He dismounted and came to the office, the strain of the last weeks showing in the deep grooved lines in his face, the weariness about his mouth and eyes. He saw Ken talking to the manager and there was only a hint of a break in his stride, a faint tightening of the lips.

He nodded distantly as Ken and the manager turned, then dropped into a chair. "They tried to burn our station at Cottonwood Bend."

Ken stared. "Who?"

"A dockworker there. Just plain luck I rode in late one night from Sioux Springs. Caught him lighting a candle he'd set in a pile of straw." Sparks' eyes glittered with vindictive pleasure. "It'll take him a month to get out of bed now that I've worked him over. Paid him equal to six months' wages to do it."

"Did you get anything to tie it to Moran?"

"Not him! Do you think he'd leave a trail? No, some hardcase in a saloon paid him to do it—and he was nowhere in the country by the time I got onto his trail. Other than that," Sparks said with bitter sarcasm, "everything's fine up north. How's it down here?"

"Nothing burned or wrecked," the manager said, "but business is dropping off. I just told Ballard here that War Bonnet is ready to cancel."

"Now that'd rip the blanket for sure! Maybe I'd better see him."

"I did," Ken said.

Sparks sank back. "Oh? And now we needn't worry?"

"I don't know. Moran's making threats, and Hayden is scared."

"Hell, I'd scare him more!" Sparks gritted.

"That's no way to handle Hayden."

"And you're a sure-fire expert on handling," Sparks said shortly.

Ken flushed, but checked his anger, biting it back. Sparks wearily passed his hand over his face and turned to the manager. "We had another teamster quit on us. Any of your men we can put at Sioux Springs?"

"I don't know. Lot of trouble up there and—"

The office door opened and all three men turned. Jeff Hayden came in, hesitated just within the door. Ken recovered first from his surprise and stepped to the barrier. "Well, Mr. Hayden!"

The man squared his shoulders. "I been thinking over what you said. Won't say I'm wrong, understand, but we'll stick to the old system for this month, at least. See how it works."

"It will," Ken said flatly.

Hayden picked up the promise. "Just to make sure, you're responsible—for both payroll and cargo."

Sparks half started up but Ken squared around to block him. "We always were. Why shouldn't we be this time?"

"I heard your insurance had been cancelled. There's risk enough in time lost, if I lose my equipment. But without insurance—"

"I haven't heard of it," Ken said firmly, and the station manager also shook his head.

Hayden looked slightly relieved. "That makes me feel better. I didn't want to go back on Lou's own flesh and blood. But with all the trouble, and what Moran hinted—"

"Moran!" Sparks spat. "A cheat and a liar."

Ken said, "When will you ship?"

"A week from today. As usual, your wagon will pick up kegs of nails for the northern mines at our warehouse."

"I know," Sparks said. "One of them will have the payroll."

"Gold coin and greenbacks." Hayden nodded. "Near five thousand dollars more than usual this time since we worked extra heavy last month." He turned to the manager. "A week from today."

"We can handle the rest, Mr. Hayden."

The mining executive opened the door, paused, looked at Ken. "Ballard, thanks for our talk. I guess I'd forgotten too many things while worrying about Moran and the War Bonnet. I confess I still do, a little. But if this goes through without a hitch, I'll know I can depend on Alice Hanes as much as I did on Lou."

He left and the manager gave a soft whistle, looked respectfully at Ken. "You did it! And I thought that customer was gone for sure!"

Sparks pulled himself from the chair. "Well, chalk one up in our favor, Ballard," he said grudgingly.

Then he turned his back on Ken as he spoke to the manager about buying supplies in Pass City for some of the outlying stations. Ken smiled tightly and left the office.

Sparks left the next morning with no further word to Ken. He was gone by the time Ken came to the station. Ken was relieved; the very presence of the man was a strain.

For the next three days Ken called on the other shippers in Pass City. Again he found that Moran had made veiled threats, given hints that the Hanes Line would be out of business within the month, that hard luck rode its wagons and cargoes. Ken countered this with the fact that War Bonnet Mining intended to stick. He swung one shipper back and the others gave half hearted, evasive promises. Ken knew all depended on the next few weeks. If, in that time, they could meet and counter anything that Moran's gunhawks and bribers threw against them, they had a chance of holding on. Just that, Ken thought, would be sufficient for now.

He rode to Sioux Springs, first checking with both the station manager and Hayden about the combined payroll-cargo shipment. The usual secrecy had been maintained, only the three men and Sparks knowing that the shipment would go out at all, and the exact date.

Alice greeted him warmly when he entered the Sioux Springs office, but within a matter of minutes Ken sensed that she was upset and unusually worried. He dropped into the chair beside her desk, grinning with a cheerfulness he didn't entirely feel.

"Whatever it is, it can't be as bad as that. We still roll a few wagons, and we held War Bonnet. We're beginning to block Moran."

She looked up and he saw the hunger for encouragement in her eyes, but also the doubt. He pressed on. "This is costing him plenty. Gunhawks don't work for nothing, and his bribes haven't been cheap. If we can block him long enough, he'll see that the cost of moving in and taking over is too high."

She sighed. "I hope you're right, but I can't believe it."

He picked up her hand. "Believe it! That's the way it's working. War Bonnet's proof."

"I wish you hadn't taken on that job."

His eyes widened in surprise. Finally he regained his voice. "Alice! It's the one shipment we need to hold!"

"I know, but if something goes wrong—outlaws, an attack—"

"We're covered. The insurance—"

"We have none. The insurance company knows what's been happening. They paid the last claim and then cancelled. If we lose anything I have to pay for it myself, Ken. I—just don't have that kind of money."

He dropped back in his chair. Then she dropped another bombshell. "Frank quit. He tried to make me fire you—said it was you or him. I tried to make him see that all of us needed you and I couldn't let you go."

She kept her eyes on her hands as she continued, speaking with some difficulty. "Frank's jealous. We've both known that—but I didn't realize how jealous. He tried to get me to marry him, said if I didn't he'd see the whole business was ruined —and you along with it."

"He's bluffing!"

"No, not Frank. I told him I wanted him to stay but I couldn't and wouldn't marry him. I thought maybe we could work it out so he'd understand and stay with us anyway. But he couldn't see beyond his jealousy, Ken. He accused you and me of . . ."

Her voice trailed off. Ken said, "He accused me first, long ago."

"Oh, I didn't know."

"I told him there was nothing. I worked a job and wanted no woman. Then, when he jumped me again, I said I was holding on to the job to pay you and your father for making me believe in people again." He paused and then plunged, suddenly seeing the wonderful truth. "But Frank was smarter than me, Alice. I didn't know it was because I just wanted—"

He broke off. Her eyes watched him, deep and warm and wondering. They confused and frightened him. Powerful memories surged up of another woman, blocking him for a moment until this new discovery dispersed the old memories.

But it was not the time to tell her. What could he offer her at this moment? Her eyes, though, told him she wanted to hear. But would it be fair to ask her now, when a hundred worries, when sorrow, pressure, and strain would make her eager for support? She had to have time to get acquainted with him, had to be free to know her own heart.

He came to his feet and spoke gruffly. "Frank will get over it. He has before. He'll be back."

"Not this time. I turned him down, and he can't stand that. He said he'd make me sorry. He was last seen talking to Brad Moran."

Ken stared. A swift succession of pictures flashed through his mind. At dawn, a freight wagon would roll slowly out of Pass City, loaded with mining supplies and equipment. One piece would be marked "keg of nails," but it would actually con-tain gold coin and greenbacks. He couldn't put on a guard; that would call atten-tion. The payroll had never been guarded before.

Sparks, twisted with jealousy and hate, knew it. He also knew that Alice was not insured as carrier. He had gone to Moran, who would instantly grasp this golden chance to smash the Hanes Line once and for all.

Ken's face grew grim and be turned on his heel and strode to the door. Alice called, "Ken! What are you going to do?"

"Find Sparks—and Moran. If I don't—"

The slamming door finished his sentence.

XX

He was halfway across the yard and almost through the gate when the girl's harassed call checked him. He whirled about and saw her coming toward him, face drawn, arm extended as though to catch and hold him.

"Ken! Please! Don't try to find them! Sparks will try to kill you, and Moran—"

Unthinking, he grasped her arms as she came up to him. "Alice, I can't just stand here. It's that payroll, don't you see?"

Her face paled and her hand came up to her mouth. She hadn't thought of it before, but now his words brought her face to face with disaster. His fingers sank deeper into the warm flesh of her arms as the barriers he had felt and feared, only moments ago in the office, suddenly vanished. He pulled her to him and kissed her. For a second she stiffened in sheer surprise and then her body surrendered to his arms. Her mouth grew soft under his lips and her arms came up around his shoulders.

They broke apart, shaken, and Ken looked hungrily into her eyes. She spoke in an emotion-choked voice. "Leave them alone. They'll try to kill you. And now that we've—"

"They have to be stopped. If they're not—"

Gently he disengaged her hands from his wrists and strode swiftly across the street, not daring to look back. He entered the hotel and pounded on the counter until the clerk appeared from his little office. From the man Ken heard that Brad Moran had left a short time ago—checked out. He had left alone.

Ken hurried to the livery stable. Moran had ridden out a short while ago. "Alone?" Ken asked.

"No," the hostler answered, "him and Frank Sparks went down the Pass City road."

Ken thanked the man and went out into the street again. He hesitated, his mind working swiftly. He thought of gathering up Hal Smith and some men at the station, but rejected that idea, doubtful if anyone but Hal himself would ride on a dangerous mission. Ken could go alone, but that would put the odds against him. He glanced toward the station where Alice waited. Life suddenly had new and rich promise, and he would not endanger that.

He recrossed the street and walked purposefully to the sheriff's office. The lawman was sorting reward dodgers at his desk and looked up in surprise when Ken entered. Then his wise eyes narrowed. "Trouble's riding with you. I can smell it."

Ken swiftly told him of the War Bonnet payroll shipment, of Sparks quitting and his threat to ruin Alice Hanes and the line, of the man's association with Brad Moran. He finished, "The two of them rode out together this morning toward Pass City."

The sheriff grunted. "I can see where the trail leads. The shipment's not guarded?"

"It never has been. One of the reasons is that there's been no trouble. Even the teamster doesn't know he hauls about twenty thousand dollars."

The sheriff pulled himself from the chair. "I reckon we'd better get some deputies."

"You need just one—me." Ken continued, as the sheriff looked surprised, "The teamster won't know Frank's not superintendent any more. He'll pull up when Sparks meets him, not suspecting a thing. Sparks will have told Moran. So why should Moran gather a bunch of gunhawks that'll arouse suspicion, when they're not needed? Just Sparks and Moran can do the job—and you can bet they won't leave a witness."

The lawman saw the point. He opened a drawer and threw a deputy badge at Ken. "Get your horse saddled and meet me here. Check your Colt and take a rifle. No telling what will come up. Ballard, I hope you're right. Ever since Lou was killed, I been wanting to pin the beatings and the fires on Moran—besides Lou's murder. This should do it."

Ken accepted the badge, then turned on his heel and hurried from the office. In half an hour the two men rode out of Sioux Springs, heading for the dark line of mountains to the south and the winding, rugged course of Treachery Pass.

They rode swiftly, covering the miles and yet not pushing their mounts too hard. Gradually the line of the mountains rose higher along the horizon. As the sun set they saw the black scar of Treachery Pass in the high rock wall of the mountains ahead. There had been no sign of Moran or Sparks; Ken figured they had pushed fast and hard.

"They want to be deep into the pass by nightfall," Ken speculated to the sheriff. "They'll find a likely place to stop the wagon when it comes through tomorrow, and then they'll camp."

"Puts them between us and the payroll, and we don't know where they'll make their play for it."

Ken nodded thoughtfully and looked toward the red-streaked sky above the jagged peaks. "When we come to the pass, let's split up. I'll ride on ahead."

"Split up!"

"They'll camp, but off the road. They'll keep hidden but, as I figure it, they'll feel safe. So they'll pay no attention to a single rider in the night, even if they hear him. That's why you and I drift through separately." Ken smiled tightly. "Means all-night riding and maybe no rest tomorrow. But it'll put us on the other side of the mountains and trailing the wagon, ready for them to hit it."

The sheriff pursed his lips, considered the plan and then lifted his reins with decision. "We'll pull off the road and have coffee and beans while we wait for full dark. Sure you want to go through first?"

Ken nodded grimly. "If they should happen to see me, you can bet they'll try to gun me down. So I'd like to feel you won't be too far behind me—a sort of ace in the hole."

They camped at the foot of the mountains, well off the road, among the trees that hid the mouth of the pass. There they built a fire and had coffee and a scant supper while the horses took a needed rest. Twilight darkened into night.

At last Ken stood up, hardly more than a moving shadow that the faintly glowing embers of the dying fire outlined. "I'll be riding."

"Give you ten minutes," the sheriff said. "If I hear shots, I'll come helling."

Ken chuckled in the night. "You do that."

He moved out, going slowly until his mount came onto the road. Then he turned the horse into the black maw of the pass, lightly touching spurs, and rode at an easy trot. The thick dust of the road muffled the steady beat of hoofs and Ken doubted if they could be heard at any distance. Besides, his unhurried pace would not arouse attention.

The tree-covered, jagged slopes surrounded him and the road seemed only a ghostly ribbon for a few yards beyond and behind him. Ken loosened the Colt in the holster, and made sure the rifle would slide easily out of its scabbard, as the horse set itself to the steepening grade.

The miles rolled behind him. He watched the dark wall of the trees, tried to pierce their shadows to distinguish the shape of a lurking rider or catch the bright flicker of a campfire somewhere in their depths.

He approached the summit, and finally the road leveled off as it curved around a high spur of the mountains. Ken heard the chilling wail of a cougar far off and, closer, the mournful cry of a coyote. Once a silent, gliding owl caused his hand to slash to his holster as he savagely reined in. A flick of shadow and the bird was gone, leaving Ken still tense, his horse skittish.

The road dipped and Ken knew he had passed the high point of the range. Still, he rode with caution around the descending loops and turns. The bright stars wheeled by slowly and gradually there was a sense of approaching dawn in the air. It came slowly, a mere seeping of light. Larger objects began to take uncertain form, then became more definite. Ken heard the first twitterings of awakening birds.

The pale, unearthly light of dawn found him well down on the southern slope of the Treacheries. Now he increased the speed of his horse. Darkness would not hide him now and there was no further need for the slow and cautious pace.

When the sun lifted above the peaks and sent bright rays into the trees, Ken drew rein at the further mouth of the pass. He knew that somewhere back of him Moran and Sparks awaited the coming of the wagon, but now Ken could consider that with a grim satisfaction. He reined off the road, dismounted, and let the horse graze while he waited for the sheriff. About now the freight wagon would be moving toward the mountains.

Nearly half an hour passed before Ken saw the sheriff ride around a turn some distance away. The lawman came up and stiffly dismounted, looking a question at Ken, who answered, "No sign of 'em."

"If they're around," the sheriff said grumpily.

"They are."

"What do we do—meet the wagon and ride guard?"

"No, we'll wait over there." Ken pointed toward bushes far back from the road. "We'll let the wagon go by, give it five minutes and then trail after it."

"They could hold it up, shoot the driver and be off with the money in five minutes."

"There are a dozen nail kegs," Ken reminded him, "and even the driver doesn't know he's carrying money. Give you odds we'll be on 'em before they've broken in the head of the first keg."

The sheriff nodded. "Let's get to the bushes, then. How long before the wagon'll be here?"

"Two hours or more."

"We'll spell one another and get some sleep, then. We could use it."

They picketed the horses behind the screen of bushes. The lawman stretched out and sought sleep, while Ken watched the road, hidden from sight himself. An hour later he roused the lawman and sought rest himself. It seemed but a moment later that the sheriff shook him.

"Thought I'd wake you. The wagon should be coming by almost any time now."

The minutes passed—a half hour, then an hour. The sheriff moved worriedly. "Reckon they might have held it up between here and Pass City?"

"I don't think so. That's open range all the way. No, they're behind us somewhere."

"I sure hope so."

"So do I!" Ken breathed, and choked back the impulse to ride out and find the wagon.

The minutes dragged on and then Ken stiffened, thinking he had heard the rattle of chains. The sheriff heard it, too. Side by side they peered through the screen of bushes. The wagon appeared around a curve, four horses set into the collars for the pull up the grade. The driver's whip cracked and the wagon rolled forward, wheeled around the curve and disappeared in a roiling cloud of dust around the next bend. Ken and the sheriff exchanged relieved looks and hurried to their horses.

They rode slowly, setting the pace of their mounts to that of the heavy wagon. Remaining well behind, they could still get faint smells off settling dust, though the cloud itself had dispersed. At each turn they moved cautiously, hands close to their guns. When they saw one stretch of road was clear, they hurried past it to the next one.

Again they approached the summit of the pass. Every hidden turn brought new tension, only to be relieved when they looked on peaceful, empty road beyond it. But the relief lasted just for a moment and the tension would build again.

Ken judged they would hit the saddle of the pass within half a mile. They rounded a turn, then rode on to the next, slowing their mounts, drifting to the curve. Ken rode slightly ahead, narrowly watching. He came into the turn, moved slowly around it and abruptly reined in, backing his horse. He signaled the sheriff to stop.

"The wagon's stopped up ahead. I saw Sparks talking to the driver."

"Moran?"

"Didn't see him. He might be drifting in from the other side while Sparks keeps the driver's attention."

"Let's leave the horses here." The sheriff swung out of saddle.

They edged forward and then Ken signaled toward the trees. Leaving the road, they cut directly across the curve. As they came on the road again, the trees thinned. Both men now carried their Colts and were moving carefully. Ken heard voices, muffled at first. Then one came clear and angry.

"Sparks, what is this? You robbing your own boss?"

"I don't work for her any more. Get down off that seat."

"There ain't nothing but hardware in this load. It ain't worth your time. Moran, I've heard bad talk about you, but I never—"

"Get down!"

Ken and the lawman moved faster as the voice came. "I'm sure goingta let 'em know what fine upstanding men you two are. You just wait until—"

"There won't be an until."

Ken and the lawman burst through the trees on a low bluff overlooking the road. Just below them, Sparks and Moran sat their horses on either side of the wagon. The teamster had half risen from the seat, face frozen in horror at the two guns leveled at him. Moran, still looking like a dapper banker, deliberately dogged back the gun hammer.

Ken lined his gun. "Hold it, Moran!"

Sparks' head jerked upward, the dark, handsome face slack in surprise. Moran sat tight and unmoving, his gun still half lifted. Without warning, he raked spurs and dropped flat on the horse's back as it bolted. He twisted about and slammed a wild shot that sang wickedly between Ken and the sheriff.

At the same moment, Sparks remembered the Colt in his hand. The weapon glinted as he jerked it up and pulled the trigger. Ken caught the movement and his own gun blurred. The sheriff's Colt roared, almost in his ears, drowning out the blast of his own gun.

An iron fist struck Ken's shoulder and he felt himself falling. He grabbed the saddlehorn and held on, fighting the spinning of his brain. Dimly he saw Sparks fold forward and then spill down the horse's flank to the ground. His senses swam and he felt that his whole left side had melted away. His fingers lost their grip on the leather and, strangely, the ground jumped up to meet him.

It seemed but a moment later that his eyes opened on a bleary and unfocused world. Gradually a white blur above him shaped into the sheriff's worried face. Ken stared blankly and then memory came with a sickening shock. He jerked erect, but a fiery cramping pain in his shoulder dropped him again.

The sheriff said, "Take it easy. You want to start that wound bleeding again?"

Ken controlled the spinning of the world and caught his voice. "The hold-up?"

"All over."

"Sparks? Moran?"

"Sparks is dead. Moran is alive, but he might as well be dead. My slug caught him in the spine. He's paralyzed." The lawman considered Ken. "We'll rest half an hour or so. I reckon you can climb into the wagon by then."

Ken nodded and closed his eyes.

He could never afterward fully remember the ride. He had vivid pictures of the immobile, dapper shape beside him in the wagon bed, a body dead except for the strangely shifting, bitter and defeated eyes. Not a sound or a word came from Moran. Ken alternated between unconsciousness and the painful jolting of the slow-moving wagon. It seemed that day had faded to night, brightened to day and merged into night again. Or it might have been the alternating of consciousness and those periods in which he was aware of nothing.

Then, coming up out of darkness, he became aware that the wagon had stopped. Moran no longer lay beside him and he saw the dark shape of men about him. Hands gently lifted him and he was lowered from the wagon.

Suddenly Alice's eyes looked into his own and he saw the fright and hope in them. He dimly knew he had to reassure her, to chase away the shadows in those beautiful eyes.

His voice seemed to come from a distance. "It's all right. Just in the shoulder. I'll get well."

"Oh, darling!" and then her lips were on his for a long electric moment.

Her slender hand felt cool and wonderful against his cheek. He had to explain. "Moran . . ."

"Sssh!" she cautioned softly. "I know. He'll never bother us again—paralyzed and with a long jail term."

"Sparks," he insisted. "I didn't want—because of you—but—"

Her hand brushed his lips, silencing them. "I wish it could have happened some other way. But don't blame yourself, Ken. The sheriff told me. Moran would have killed you."

Ken looked up at her for a long moment and then sighed, a long, soft sound. "I never thought there'd be another woman . . . but you . . ."

"Me," she repeated firmly. "And none other for you, ever again. That's an order."

He smiled and held her hand as men lifted the improvised stretcher and carried him across the lantern-lit station yard.

His mind drifted for a moment, but now there was a curing peace in the darkness, and her firm fingers grasping him were promise of a new life beyond this strange world of half sleep and receding pain. He became aware that the motion had stopped and his brain struggled up out of torpor.

He heard her voice. ". . . to my house, Doctor. I'll nurse him and see he gets well. I have to. I want to marry him, when he gets around to asking me."

He had to do that—now! This time . . . his mind drifted into darkness again. But he was content. It was a healing and passing darkness.

Center Point Large Print
600 Brooks Road / PO Box 1
Thorndike, ME 04986-0001 USA

(207) 568-3717

US & Canada:
1 800 929-9108
www.centerpointlargeprint.com